# LIVES AND
# DEATHS

LEO TOLSTOY

# LIVES AND DEATIIS

## ESSENTIAL STORIES

Translated from the Russian
by Boris Dralyuk

PUSHKIN PRESS
LONDON

Pushkin Press
71–75 Shelton Street
London WC2H 9JQ

English translation © 2019 Boris Dralyuk

*The Death of Ivan Ilyich* was first published as 'Smert' Ivana Il'icha'
(Смерть Ивана Ильича) in *Sochineniia gr. L. N. Tolstogo*, Part XII (Moscow, 1886)

'Pace-setter: The Story of a Horse' was first published as
'Kholstomer. Istoriia loshadi' (Холстомер. История лошади)
in *Sochineniia gr. L. N. Tolstogo*, Part III (Moscow, 1886)

'Three Deaths' was first published as 'Tri smerti'
(Три смерти) in *Biblioteka dlia chteniia*, No. 1 (1859)

'Alyosha the Pot' was first published as 'Alesha Gorshok'
(Алёша Горшок) in *Posmertnye khudozhestvennye proizvedeniia
L. N. Tolstogo*, Vol. I, ed. V. G. Chertkov (Moscow, 1911)

This translation first published by Pushkin Press in 2019

1 3 5 7 9 8 6 4 2

ISBN 13: 978-1-78227-541-1

Frontispiece: Count Leo Nikolayevich Tolstoy (1828–1910) the
Russian writer, aesthetic philosopher, moralist and mystic inspecting
the estate after a bathe in the lake © Hulton Archive / Stringer

Designed and typeset by Tetragon, London
Printed and bound in Great Britain by TJ International,
Padstow, Cornwall on Munken Premium White 80gsm

www.pushkinpress.com

# CONTENTS

# TRANSLATOR'S PREFACE

THE PROSPECT of writing briefly about Count Leo Nikolayevich Tolstoy (1828 1910)—whose life spanned nearly a century of political changes and fervent intellectual debate in Russia and abroad, and whose complete works occupy 90 austere volumes (with a new 100-volume edition now in preparation)—is daunting indeed.[1] Still more daunting is the prospect of selecting and translating his "essential stories". At first, the word "essential" lent a heartening clarity to the mission, for it was perfectly obvious to me that no subject was more essential to Tolstoy's work than that of death. But soon I was in the dark again. After all, as the Russian émigré author Mark Aldanov (1886–1957) wrote some years after Tolstoy's own uneasy demise at a train station, no other writer had ever before amassed such a "treasure chest" of artistic depictions of death.[2] And even if we take the novels and spiritual writings out of consideration, we are still left with a wealth of novellas and stories that grapple with the essence of life in its final moments.

As I read and reread the stories, however, patterns began to emerge, and with them a more definite goal. I wanted to present writing from every stage of Tolstoy's career—early, middle and late—that would trace the author's continued, evolving, all-consuming engagement with the twinned questions of what makes for a good life and what makes for a good death. I also wanted to highlight what I believe to be the heart of Tolstoy's artistic gift, the breathtaking fearlessness of his imagination, which allowed him both to approach what most of us are unwilling to ponder and to thrill us with his depiction of it, rendering us incapable of turning away.

It seemed only natural that the collection should open with *The Death of Ivan Ilyich* (1886), the title of which announces its focus in no uncertain terms. The consummately "decent" (not a laudatory term in Tolstoy's lexicon) life that leads to the protagonist's painful death is sketched out with an efficiency that can fairly be described as ruthless, while the death itself unfolds slowly; we are made to taste, though not to savour it. The novella is difficult to read, and difficult to translate—for that requires a much slower, more careful reading—but it is impossible to forget.

However one understands the judgement meted out to Ivan Ilyich, and regardless of whether one agrees with or rebels against it, one is changed forever by the trial.[3]

The second tale in the volume, which I have titled "Pace-setter: The Story of Horse",[4] bridges two phases of Tolstoy's creative life. Begun in 1863, it lay dormant until 1885, when the author's wife discovered the manuscript among his papers and encouraged him to prepare it for publication. For this, and for much else, we owe Sofia Tolstaya a great debt; in its final version, "Pace-setter" is a remarkable feat of empathy and invention. While the narrative of Ivan Ilyich burrows inwards, growing ever more narrow, the story of Pace-setter expands in wholly unexpected ways, offering us a fresh—if not refreshing—perspective on our world.[5]

Remarkably, this power to freshen our vision was available to Tolstoy from the start. It is already on display in the closing section of "Three Deaths", a brief story written over the course of a few days in 1858. I will not spoil the effect of its ending by discussing it here, but I will say that I chose to include the story because its core concerns are echoed in much of the author's later work: the tension between our earthly desires and our spiritual needs; between faith and religion; between the ways of the common folk and those of the civilized elite; and between the realm of humanity and the realm of nature.

Whether these tensions were productively resolved by Tolstoy after his religious awakening in the late 1870s—or, indeed, whether they can ever be resolved—is an open one. But near the end of his life Tolstoy came strikingly close to portraying, in just a few pages, the resolution of all tension. D.S. Mirsky, the great historian of Russian literature, calls Tolstoy's "Alyosha the Pot" (1905) "a masterpiece of rare perfection". Its titular hero, Mirsky writes, is "a peasant boy who was all his life everyone's drudge but, in his simplicity of soul and meek, unquestioning submission (non-resistance) knew that inner light and purity of conscience, that perfect peace, which was never attained by the conscious, rational, restless soul of Tolstoy".[6]

It is my hope that this collection charts Tolstoy's restless, lifelong, perhaps tragic yet eternally resonant search for an inner light.

# LIVES AND DEATHS

# THE DEATH OF
# IVAN ILYICH

I

I N THE LARGE BUILDING that housed the halls of
justice, during an adjournment in the Melvinsky
trial, the members of the court and the public prosecutor gathered in the office of Ivan Yegorovich Shebek.
Their talk soon turned to the famous Krasovsky case.
Fyodor Vasilyevich grew heated, insisting on the
manifest lack of jurisdiction, Ivan Yegorovich wasn't
swayed, while Pyotr Ivanovich, who had kept out
of the fray from the start, leafed through the latest
issue of the *Gazette*, which had just been delivered.

"Gentlemen," he interrupted, "Ivan Ilyich is dead."

"Can't be…"

"Here, have a look," he replied, handing the fresh,
still pungent pages to Fyodor Vasilyevich.

The announcement was bordered in black: "It
is with deepest sorrow that Praskovya Fyodorovna

Golovina informs relatives and friends of the demise of her beloved spouse, Member of the Appellate Court Ivan Ilyich Golovin, which occurred on 4th February 1882. The funeral will be held on Friday, at one o'clock in the afternoon."

Ivan Ilyich had been a colleague of the assembled gentlemen, well liked by all of them. He had been ill for several weeks; they had heard the illness was incurable. His position had been kept open, but it was assumed that, in the event of his death, Alekseyev would be appointed to replace him, while Alekseyev's position would be filled by either Vinnikov or Stabel. And so, upon learning of Ivan Ilyich's death, the first thought that occurred to each of the gentlemen gathered in the office concerned the potential reassignments or promotions that this death might occasion for the members themselves or for their acquaintances.

*Now I'll surely be named to replace Stabel or Vinnikov,* thought Fyodor Vasilyevich. *They've been promising me a promotion for a long time. And it means a raise of eight hundred roubles, along with an allowance.*

*I'll have to apply for my brother-in-law's transfer from Kaluga,* thought Pyotr Ivanovich. *Yes, that ought to make my wife very happy indeed. No more complaints about my never doing anything for her family.*

"I sensed he was a goner," Pyotr Ivanovich stated. "A pity."

"What was it, anyway?"

"The doctors couldn't say, exactly. That is, they all said different things. When I last saw him, it looked like he might still recover."

"I hadn't seen him since the holidays myself, though I kept meaning to visit…"

"Did he have much property?"

"I think his wife has a little. Hardly anything."

"Well, we'll have to go, I suppose. They lived so terribly far away."

"You mean so terribly far from you. You're far from everything."

"See? He'll never forgive me for moving to the other side of the river," Pyotr Ivanovich said, smiling at Shebck. And so, speaking of distances between this and that part of the city, they made their way back to the hearing.

In addition to considerations of transfers and other potential career changes that this particular death might bring about, the very fact of the death of a close acquaintance prompted in each person who learnt of it, as such things always do, a joyous sense that it was he who had died, and not they.

*Dead. He's dead*, each of them thought, *but I'm not.* And Ivan Ilyich's closest acquaintances, his so-called friends, had another thought: it occurred to them, involuntarily, that they would now have to fulfil the dreary obligations of decorum, attending his funeral and paying his widow a visit of condolence.

Fyodor Vasilyevich and Pyotr Ivanovich had been closer to him than anyone.

Pyotr Ivanovich had known Ivan Ilyich since their days at law school, and he considered himself beholden to the man.

After informing his wife over dinner of his colleague's death and of the possibility of his brother-in-law's transfer to their district, Pyotr Ivanovich forewent his nap, put on his tailcoat, and drove to Ivan Ilyich's residence.

A carriage and two cabs stood at the entrance to Ivan Ilyich's apartment. In the downstairs hallway, resting against the wall by the coat stand, was a glazed brocade coffin lid trimmed with tassels and a braid that had been polished with powder. Two ladies in black were removing their furs. Pyotr Ivanovich recognized one of them—Ivan Ilyich's sister—but not the other. His colleague Schwartz was about to descend the stairs, but when he saw Pyotr Ivanovich he paused on the top step and winked, as if to say:

*Ivan Ilyich made rather a mess of things; you and I would have handled this differently.*

Schwartz's face, with its English whiskers, and the whole of his lanky figure in its tailcoat, had, as usual, an air of elegant solemnity, and this solemnity, which always stood in such stark contrast to Schwartz's playfulness, was particularly piquant under these circumstances. So thought Pyotr Ivanovich.

Pyotr Ivanovich allowed the ladies to go ahead of him and slowly followed them to the stairs. Schwartz stayed where he was. Pyotr Ivanovich understood why: he wanted to make arrangements for their bridge game that evening. The ladies proceeded up the stairs to the widow, while Schwartz, with his strong, sternly pressed lips and his playful gaze, twitched his eyebrows to point Pyotr Ivanovich to the right, in the direction of the dead man's room.

Pyotr Ivanovich entered, at a loss as to what he should do, as everyone always is in such cases. Of one thing he was certain: it's never a bad idea to cross oneself. But he wasn't entirely sure about bowing, so he compromised: he entered the room crossing himself and bowing ever so slightly. Meanwhile, as far as his arms and head allowed him, he looked around the room. Two young men, one still in high school—nephews, in all likelihood—were moving towards the door, still crossing themselves. An old woman stood motionless. A lady with strangely arched eyebrows was saying something to her in a whisper. An alert, resolute lector in a frock coat was reading something in a loud voice with an expression that suggested he would brook no contradiction. The butler's helper, Gerasim, passed before Pyotr Ivanovich with light steps and sprinkled something on the floor; as soon as Pyotr Ivanovich saw this, he became aware of the faint scent of a decaying corpse. On his last visit to Ivan Ilyich, Pyotr Ivanovich had seen this peasant, this Gerasim, in his colleague's study; the fellow had been acting as his master's nurse, and Ivan Ilyich was especially fond of him. Pyotr Ivanovich kept crossing himself and bowing slightly, aiming at a spot between the coffin, the lector and the icons on the table in the corner. Then, when he felt this crossing movement had gone on too long, he stopped and turned to examine the dead man.

The dead man lay, as dead men always lie, in the uniquely heavy manner of dead men, with his stiff limbs sunk into the lining of the coffin and his head bowed, for all time, on the pillow; his waxen yellow brow, with bald spots at the hollow temples, was thrust forward, as it always is with dead men, and his protruding nose appeared to be pressing down on his upper lip. He had changed quite a lot, had grown even thinner since Pyotr Ivanovich had seen him last, but his face, like all dead faces, was more beautiful, and, above all, more imposing than it had been in life. The expression it bore indicated that what needed to be done had been done, and had been done right. What was more, the expression contained a reproach or reminder to the living. Pyotr Ivanovich found this reminder to be inappropriate or, at the very least, inapplicable to himself. He was suddenly ill at ease, and so he crossed himself once more, hastily, and then—too hastily, it seemed to him, to be consistent with decorum—turned towards the door and left. Schwartz was waiting in the passage room, legs wide apart, both hands toying with his top hat behind his back. A single glance at Schwartz's playful, well-groomed, elegant figure refreshed Pyotr Ivanovich; he realized that Schwartz stood above all this, that he would never allow this to depress him. His very appearance suggested that the incident of Ivan Ilyich's service could in no way provide sufficient cause to disrupt the procedure of the meeting, that is, that nothing could prevent them from snapping open a new deck of cards that very evening, while a footman brought in four fresh candles; in general, there was no reason to suppose that this incident would prevent them from enjoying the evening together. That's precisely what he said, in a whisper, as Pyotr Ivanovich passed by, proposing they meet at Fyodor Vasilyevich's. But fate seemed to be conspiring against the prospect of cards that evening. Praskovya Fyodorovna—a short, fat woman, who, despite all her efforts to achieve the opposite, grew steadily wider from the shoulders down—dressed all in black, her head covered with lace, with the same strangely arched eyebrows as the woman by the coffin, emerged from her rooms with a group of ladies, led them to the dead man's door and announced: "The service is about to begin; please, do go through."

Schwartz gave a vague bow and remained where he was, apparently neither accepting nor rejecting the invitation. Recognizing Pyotr Ivanovich, Praskovya Fyodorovna sighed, came close, took him by the hand and said: "I know you were a true friend of Ivan Ilyich…" She looked at him, expecting actions that would correspond to her words.

Just as Pyotr Ivanovich had known that it was necessary to cross himself in the dead man's room, so did he know that it was now necessary to press the woman's hand, sigh and say: "Believe me…" And so that is what he did, and by doing it, he felt he had achieved the desired result: both he and she were touched.

"Come, let us go before it starts; we must have a talk," said the widow. "Give me your arm."

Pyotr Ivanovich surrendered his arm and they went to the inner rooms, passing Schwartz, who gave Pyotr Ivanovich a mournful wink: *There goes your game of bridge, old chap. Don't be offended if we find someone to take your spot. If you manage to slip away, do join us as the fifth*, said his playful look.

Pyotr Ivanovich sighed yet more deeply and mournfully, and Praskovya Fyodorovna pressed his arm in gratitude. They entered her drawing room, which was upholstered in pink cretonne and lit by a dim lamp, and sat down at the table—she on the sofa, he on a low pouf with loose springs that yielded awkwardly beneath him. Praskovya Fyodorovna had wanted to warn him about the pouf and direct him to another chair, but she had changed her mind, thinking that such a warning would have been inappropriate for a woman in her position. As he lowered himself onto the pouf, Pyotr Ivanovich recalled how much care Ivan Ilyich had taken in decorating this room, how he had sought his opinion about this very pink cretonne with green leaves. As the widow moved towards the couch (the

whole room was stuffed with knick-knacks and furniture), the black lace of her black shawl caught on
the carved edge of the table. Pyotr Ivanovich rose
to help her, liberating the pouf, which rumbled and
gave him a push. The widow began to detach the
shawl herself, and Pyotr Ivanovich sat back down,
again suppressing the rebellious pouf. But the widow
didn't manage to free the shawl completely, so Pyotr
Ivanovich rose once more, at which point the pouf
rebelled again and even gave a pop. When all this
was finally over, the widow took out a clean cambric
handkerchief and began to cry. The episode with
the lace and the battle against the pouf had cooled
Pyotr Ivanovich's feelings considerably, and he sat
frowning. This uncomfortable situation was interrupted by Sokolov, Ivan Ilyich's butler, who came in
to report that the burial plot Praskovya Fyodorovna
had designated would cost two hundred roubles. She
stopped crying, glanced at Pyotr Ivanovich with an
expression of victimhood, and said, in French, that
this was all very difficult for her. Pyotr Ivanovich
responded with a silent gesture that was meant to
express his utter certainty that this must indeed be
the case.

"Please do smoke," she said in a beneficent yet
dejected voice, and began to discuss the price of

plots with Sokolov. Lighting up, Pyotr Ivanovich heard her enquiring very thoroughly about various prices before making a final decision. And then, having settled the matter of the plot, she dealt with the question of the choir. Sokolov left.

"I see to everything myself," she told Pyotr Ivanovich, pushing aside the albums that lay between them. Then, noticing that his ashes threatened the table, she hastily moved an ashtray towards him and said: "It would be false to affirm that grief prevents me from dealing with practical affairs. Quite the opposite; if anything can—I won't say comfort… distract me, it's taking care of him." She again took out her handkerchief, as if she were about to cry, but suddenly, as if overcoming her emotion, she shook herself and spoke calmly: "But there is something you and I must discuss."

Pyotr Ivanovich bowed, but was careful to keep control over the springs of the pouf, which had begun to stir beneath him.

"He suffered terribly in his last days."

"Was it very terrible?" asked Pyotr Ivanovich.

"Terrible! He screamed and screamed, not for minutes, but for hours on end. For three whole days he screamed without stopping. It was unbearable. I honestly don't know how I endured it—you could hear him screaming through three closed doors. Oh, the things I was forced to endure!"

"And can it be that he was conscious the whole time?" asked Pyotr Ivanovich.

"Yes," she whispered, "up to the very last minute. He said his goodbyes a quarter of an hour before he passed, and even asked that Volodya be taken away."

Despite the unpleasant awareness of his and this woman's insincerity, the thought of the suffering of a man he had known so intimately, first as a cheerful young boy, a schoolmate, then in adulthood, as a colleague, struck horror into Pyotr Ivanovich's mind. He saw that brow again, that nose pressing down on the upper lip, and felt fear for himself.

*Three days of terrible suffering followed by death. But that could happen to me, at any minute*, he thought, and, for a moment, grew frightened. But that very second— and he himself did not know how—he was relieved by the customary thought that this had happened to Ivan Ilyich, not to him, and that it neither should nor could happen to him; to think otherwise would be to succumb to depression, which one mustn't do, as Schwartz's face had clearly indicated. And having reached this reasoned conclusion, Pyotr Ivanovich grew calm and began to enquire with interest about the details of Ivan Ilyich's demise, as if death were an experience peculiar to Ivan Ilyich and entirely foreign to himself.

After going over the details of Ivan Ilyich's truly terrible physical suffering (details that Pyotr Ivanovich learnt only by means of their effect on the nerves of Praskovya Fyodorovna), the widow evidently found it necessary to get down to business.

"Oh, Pyotr Ivanovich, how hard it is... How terribly, terribly hard..." And her tears came again.

Pyotr Ivanovich sighed and waited as she blew her nose. When she had finished blowing her nose he said, "Believe me..." At which point she began to talk again, and finally got around to what was, apparently, her primary concern in seeing him; this was the question of how to secure money from the Treasury on the occasion of her husband's death. She made it seem as if she were asking Pyotr Ivanovich's advice about her pension, but he saw that she already knew, to the smallest detail, what he himself did not know—just how much could be extracted from the Treasury on the occasion of this death; what she wanted to know now was whether she could somehow extract a bit more money. Pyotr Ivanovich tried to come up with some means of doing so, but, after giving it some thought and, for propriety's sake, rebuking our government for its stinginess, he said it seemed no more could be got. At this she sighed and evidently began to look for some means to get rid of her visitor. He understood this, put out his cigarette, got up, pressed her hand and went out into the hallway.

In the dining room, where Ivan Ilyich had placed the clock that he was so delighted to have bought at an antique shop, Pyotr Ivanovich met the priest and several other acquaintances who had come for the service, and also spotted the familiar face of a beautiful young lady, Ivan Ilyich's daughter. She was dressed all in black. Her waist, which had always been thin, seemed still thinner. The look on her face was gloomy, resolute, almost angry, and the way she bowed to Pyotr Ivanovich, it was as if he were guilty of something. Behind her, also looking offended, stood a rich young man whom Pyotr Ivanovich recognized, an examining magistrate—the daughter's fiancé, he had heard. Pyotr Ivanovich gave them a mournful bow and wanted to proceed to the dead man's room when, from under the stairs, appeared the little figure of Ivan Ilyich's son, still a schoolboy, who bore an uncanny resemblance to his father. He was, for all the world, a little Ivan Ilyich, just as Pyotr Ivanovich remembered him from their law school days. His tear-stained eyes were such as one finds in impure boys of thirteen or fourteen. Upon seeing Pyotr Ivanovich, the boy grimly and bashfully knitted his brow. Pyotr Ivanovich nodded to him and entered the dead man's room. The service began: candles, moans, incense, tears, sobs. Pyotr Ivanovich stood frowning, looking at the legs in front of him. He never once glanced at the dead man, yielded to no weakening influences, and was one of the first to leave. The downstairs hallway was empty. Gerasim, the butler's helper, popped out of the dead man's room, rummaged through all the coats with his strong hands, found Pyotr Ivanovich's and gave it to him.

"Well, brother Gerasim?" said Pyotr Ivanovich, so as to say something. "A pity, isn't it?"

"God's will. We're all bound for the same end," said Gerasim, baring his solid white peasant teeth; then, like a man swept up in hard work, he briskly opened the door, called to the coachman, helped Pyotr Ivanovich in, and leapt back to the porch, looking as if he were searching for something else to do.

Pyotr Ivanovich found the clean air especially pleasant after the smell of the incense, the corpse, and the carbolic acid.

"Where to?" asked the coachman.

LEO TOLSTOY

"Not too late, really. I think I'll drop in on Fyodor Vasilyevich."

And so Pyotr Ivanovich drove to Fyodor Vasilyevich's, where he found the others finishing the first rubber, a perfect time for him to cut in as the fifth.

II

The finished story of Ivan Ilyich's life was a most simple and ordinary one, and most terrible.

Ivan Ilyich, a member of the Appellate Court, died at forty-five. He was the son of an official who had made a career in Petersburg in various ministries and departments—the sort of career that brings people to a point at which, though they are clearly unfit for any significant position, they can no longer, on account of their long service and rank, be driven out, and are therefore given fictitious posts attached to factual salaries of anywhere between six and ten thousand, which accompany them to a ripe old age.

Such was the privy councillor and useless member of various useless institutions Ilya Efimovich Golovin.

He had three sons, of whom Ivan Ilyich was the second. The eldest had made the same career as his father, only at a different ministry, and was already nearing the age at which one obtained this plateau of salary. The third son was a disappointment. He had made a mess of things in a number of posts and was now working for the railways: both his father and brothers, and especially their wives, not only did not like to see him, but even avoided acknowledging his existence unless it was absolutely necessary. Their sister had married Baron Greff, a Petersburg official of their father's type. Ivan Ilyich was *le phénix de la famille*, as they said. He was neither as cold and prim as the eldest brother, nor as reckless as the youngest. He was, in fact, a happy medium—an intelligent, lively, pleasant and all-round decent person. He and his younger brother both studied law, but the latter was expelled from the fifth class; Ivan Ilyich, on the other hand, successfully completed the course. By the time he was in law school, he was already the man he would be for the rest of his life: capable, jolly, good-natured and sociable, but strictly committed to fulfilling what he considered to be his duty; and what he considered to be his duty was what people in high places considered it to be. He wasn't a lickspittle—neither as a boy nor as an adult—but there was this about him: from a very young age, he was drawn, like a fly to the light, to people in high places, adopting their attitudes, their views on life, and establishing friendly relations with them. All the fancies of childhood and youth had passed without leaving much of a trace; he had given himself over to sensuality, to vanity, and—towards the end, in the senior classes—to liberalism, but all within certain limits, which had been accurately set by his innate good sense.

In law school he did certain things that had formerly seemed truly vile to him, and he had felt disgusted with himself as he did them; but in later years, when he saw that these same things were done by people of high standing, who didn't regard them as bad at all, he was able not so much to regard them as good as to block them from his mind, and he was no longer troubled by memories of having done them.

Having graduated from law school in the tenth rank of the civil service,[1] Ivan Ilyich received from his father a sum of money for a suit of clothes, which he ordered from Charmeur,[2] affixed a little medallion inscribed "*respice finem*" to his watch chain, said his goodbyes to his tutor and the school's patron prince, dined with his friends at Donon's[3] and—with his new fashionable suitcase, linens, clothing, shaving kit, toiletries and travelling rug, all ordered and purchased from the finest shops—left for the provinces to take up the position his father had secured for him with the local governor, as an official for special assignments.[4]

In the provinces Ivan Ilyich immediately arranged for himself a routine that was as easy and pleasant as the one he had enjoyed in law school. He did his work, advancing his career, while also finding time for pleasant, decent amusements; occasionally he was sent to this or that district on assignment, mostly concerning the Old Believers,[5] and he always behaved towards both his superiors and inferiors with utmost dignity, performing his duties with a degree of accuracy and incorruptible honesty in which he could not help but take pride.

In official circumstances, he was, despite his youth and penchant for light amusement, extremely reserved, formal and even severe; but in society he was often witty and playful, as well as unfailingly amiable, decent and, in the words of the governor and his wife, who treated him like one of the family, a *bon enfant*.

There was, in the provinces, an affair with one of the local ladies, who had all but thrown herself at the dandified lawyer; there was also a modiste; there were drinking bouts with visiting adjutants and excursions to a certain backstreet after supper; and there was a degree of toadying to his chief, and even to the chief's wife—but all this had about it such a high tone of decency that no strong words were in order. It all came under the French heading of "*Il faut que jeunesse se passe*". It was all done with clean hands, in clean shirts, with French words and, most importantly, in the most rarefied realms of society, hence, with the approval of people of high standing.

Such was Ivan Ilyich's working life for five years, and then came a change. New judicial institutions had appeared; new people were needed to staff them.

Ivan Ilyich became one of these new men.

He was offered the post of examining magistrate, and he accepted it, despite the fact that it meant moving to another province, abandoning the relations he had established and establishing new ones. Ivan Ilyich's friends gave him a proper send-off, sitting for a group photo and presenting him with a silver cigarette case. And he left to take up his new post.

As an examining magistrate Ivan Ilyich was every bit as *comme il faut*—every bit as decent, as perfectly capable of separating his duties from his private life and of inspiring general respect—as he had been in the role of official for special assignments.

The work of examining magistrate, however, proved much more interesting and attractive to Ivan Ilyich than his previous occupation. In his old job he had found it pleasant to don his Charmeur uniform and stroll casually past crowds of trembling petitioners and envious officials straight into the chief's office, where he would sit down for tea and a cigarette. But there were few people over whom he had any real power, few who truly depended on him—only police officers and the Old Believers, when he was out on assignment; and he liked to deal with these people, these dependants of his, politely, in an almost comradely fashion, liked to make them feel that he, who had the power to crush them, was treating them like a friend. There weren't many such people back then. Now, as an examining magistrate, Ivan Ilyich sensed that he had power over everyone, without exception—even over the most important and self-satisfied of people; all he had to do was to write a few formulaic words on official headed paper and some important, self-satisfied individual would be hauled in before him as a defendant or witness and forced to answer his questions, and if Ivan Ilyich should choose not to offer a chair, that individual would remain standing. Ivan Ilyich never abused this power and, on the

contrary, tried to soften its effect; but his awareness of this power and the ability to soften it were
precisely what made his new work so interesting and
attractive. And when it came to the work itself—that
is, to his examinations—Ivan Ilyich very quickly
learnt to distance himself from all considerations
that did not directly affect the matter at hand and
to present even the most complicated of cases in
such a form that only the case's external aspects
would find their way onto paper, completely free
of his personal opinion and, most importantly, in
accordance with all required formalities. This was
a new way of doing things. Indeed, he had been
one of the first people to work out in practice the
application of the judicial reforms of 1864.

On moving to a new town and taking up the
post of examining magistrate, Ivan Ilyich made
new acquaintances and connections, put himself
on a rather different footing and adopted a slightly
different tone. He now distanced himself from the
provincial authorities, surrounding himself instead
with the town's finest legal minds and wealthiest
nobles. His tone was now one of mild discontent
with the government, moderate liberalism and
enlightened citizenship. At the same time, without
at all compromising the elegance of his attire, Ivan

Ilyich now stopped shaving his chin and gave free rein to his beard.

And Ivan Ilyich's life in this new town was no less pleasant than it had been in the old one: his social circle, in which it was fashionable to complain of the local governor, was friendly and kind, his salary was higher, and he derived no small pleasure from whist, a game he took up with relish. Ivan Ilyich, as it happens, was a cheerful, quick-witted and quite subtle card player, and so he generally came out ahead.

After two years of service in this new town, Ivan Ilyich met his future wife. Praskovya Fyodorovna Mikhel was the most attractive, clever and polished young woman of the circle in which he revolved; and so, among other diversions and relaxations from his professional labours, Ivan Ilyich established a light, playful relationship with her.

As an official for special assignments, Ivan Ilyich used to dance quite a bit, but now, as an examining magistrate, he only did so on occasion. These days he danced exclusively in order to prove that, although he served in the new institutions and had reached the fifth rank, if you were looking for a dancer, you wouldn't find a better one than Ivan Ilyich. And so, at the end of an evening, he would sometimes dance with Praskovya Fyodorovna, and it was primarily during these dances that he captured the lady's heart. She fell in love. Ivan Ilyich had had no clear, definite intention of getting married, but when the girl fell in love, he asked himself a question. The question was: *Well, why shouldn't I marry?*

Praskovya Fyodorovna came of a fine noble family; she wasn't bad looking and had a bit of property. Ivan Ilyich could have pursued a more brilliant match, but this one was perfectly suitable. He had his salary, and she, he hoped, would contribute just as much. Here was a sweet, pretty, altogether decent young lady, with good connections. To say that Ivan Ilyich married because he had fallen in love with his bride and found that she sympathized with his views on life would be as unfair as to say that he married because the people in his set approved of the match. In truth, Ivan Ilyich was influenced by both considerations: his new wife brought him personal happiness and, at the same time, he had done what was considered right and proper by people of high standing.

And so Ivan Ilyich got married.

The actual process of getting married, as well as the early days of marital life, with its conjugal caresses, new furniture, new crockery, new linens, went very well indeed, before his wife's pregnancy.

In fact, Ivan Ilyich came to feel that marriage would not only fail to violate the nature of his easy, pleasant, cheerful, always decent and respectable life—which he considered to be the proper nature of life in general—but would even enhance it. But then, in the very first months of his wife's pregnancy, there appeared something new, unexpected, unpleasant, difficult and altogether indecent, which could not have been anticipated and from which he could not escape.

Without any cause, as it seemed to Ivan Ilyich—*de gaité de cœur*, as he said to himself—his wife began to violate their pleasant, decent course of life. For no reason at all, she became jealous and began to demand his constant attention, to find fault with everything he did and to make crude and unpleasant scenes.

At first Ivan Ilyich had hoped to free himself of this unpleasant situation with that same easy and decent attitude towards life that had previously stood him in such good stead. He attempted to ignore his wife's moods and continue to live as easily and pleasantly as before; he'd invite people over for a game of cards, try to go to the club or visit his friends. But one time his wife began to scold him so energetically and with such crude words, and then continued to scold him so persistently whenever he failed to fulfil her demands, having obviously decided not to stop until he submitted—in other words, until he agreed to stay at home, languishing, just like her—that Ivan Ilyich grew scared. He realized that matrimony—at least with Praskovya Fyodorovna—did not always further the pleasures and decency of life but, on the contrary, often violated them, and so one had to guard oneself against these violations. Ivan Ilyich began to search for means of doing so. His work was the one thing that impressed Praskovya Fyodorovna; it was with the help of his work and its ensuing obligations that Ivan Ilyich began to contend against his wife, erecting barriers around his own independent world.

The need for these barriers became all the more pressing with the birth of their child, the troubled attempts to feed it, and the real and imaginary illnesses of both child and mother, which required Ivan Ilyich to sympathize but remained a total mystery to him.

As his wife became more and more irritable and demanding, Ivan Ilyich increasingly shifted his life's centre of gravity towards his official duties. He began to draw greater pleasure from his work and grew more ambitious.

Very soon, no more than a year after his wedding, Ivan Ilyich came to realize that marriage, though it presented certain comforts in life, was in fact a very complicated, difficult affair—and that in order to fulfil his duty, that is, to lead a decent life that met with society's approval, it was necessary to develop a particular attitude towards wedlock, as one does towards work.

And so Ivan Ilyich developed such an attitude. He demanded of family life only the comforts it could reasonably provide—supper, housekeeping, bed and, most importantly, superficial decorum, as defined by public opinion. As to the rest, he merely sought cheerful pleasure, and, should he find it, was very grateful; if, on the other hand, he should meet with resistance and grumbling, he would at once withdraw into his separate world of work, around which he had erected his barriers and in which pleasure was easily found.

Ivan Ilyich was valued as a good official, and after three years he was made assistant prosecutor. The new duties, their importance, the ability to haul anyone into court or lock them up in jail, the publicity that greeted his speeches, the success Ivan Ilyich attained—all this made his work that much more appealing.

They had more children. His wife grew more and more querulous and ill-tempered, but the attitude

Ivan Ilyich had developed towards his domestic life made him almost impervious to her grumbling.

After seven years of service in the same town, Ivan Ilyich was appointed prosecutor in another province. They moved. Money was tight, and his wife didn't like the new place. His salary was higher, but life was more expensive; in addition, two of his children died, and so family life became even more unpleasant for Ivan Ilyich.

Praskovya Fyodorovna blamed her husband for all the misfortunes that befell them in this new town. Most of the topics of conversation between husband and wife, especially those concerning the children's upbringing, eventually led back to the causes of past quarrels, and these same quarrels were ready to flare up at any moment. Now only brief spells of amorousness remained. These were islets at which they would moor for a time, only to set sail again upon a sea of deep-seated resentment that found expression in their estrangement from one another. This estrangement might have upset Ivan Ilyich, had he believed that things should be otherwise. By then, however, he had come to regard this situation as not only normal, but as the very goal of his conduct in the family. His goal was to free himself more and more from these troubles and to lend them the appearance of harmlessness and decency; he achieved it by spending less and less time with his family, and whenever he couldn't escape their company, he tried to secure his position with the presence of outsiders. The main thing was that Ivan Ilyich had his job. His whole interest in life was concentrated in the world of work, and this interest absorbed him. Consciousness of his power, of his ability to ruin any person he wished to ruin, the dignity, even superficially, with which he entered court and met with his subordinates, his success with his superiors and inferiors and, most importantly, the mastery with which he felt he conducted his affairs—all this brought him joy, and, together with companionable chats, dinners and whist, made his life complete. And so, in general, Ivan Ilyich's life proceeded as he believed it should proceed: pleasantly and decently.

Another seven years passed in this fashion. His eldest daughter was already sixteen, another child had died and only one son was left, a schoolboy, the subject of contention. Ivan Ilyich had wanted to send him to the law school, but Praskovya Fyodorovna, to spite her husband, enrolled the boy in the high school. The daughter was taking lessons at home and was turning out well. The son, too, was a fair student.

## III

Such was the course of Ivan Ilyich's life for the seventeen years following his marriage. He was already a veteran prosecutor, who had refused certain transfers in anticipation of a more desirable post, when suddenly an unpleasant circumstance disturbed his peaceful existence. Ivan Ilyich had been expecting to be named presiding judge in a university town, but Hoppe somehow leapt ahead of him and secured the post instead. This chafed Ivan Ilyich. He reproached Hoppe, quarrelled with him and with his immediate superiors; they began to treat Ivan Ilyich coolly, and when it came time to make another appointment, he was passed over again.

This was in 1880, the most difficult year of Ivan Ilyich's life, when it turned out, on the one hand, that his salary wasn't sufficient for the family to live on, and on the other, that everyone had forgotten all about him, and that what seemed to him to be the cruellest, most egregious injustice was to others quite an ordinary turn of events. Even his father did not consider it his duty to lend a helping hand. Ivan Ilyich felt that everyone had abandoned him, considering his position, with its 3,500-rouble salary, to be entirely normal and even generous. Only he and he alone knew that with the consciousness of the injustices done to him, with his wife's incessant henpecking, and with the debts he had taken on by living above his means, his situation was far from normal.

That summer, to lighten his expenses, he took a leave of absence and went with Praskovya Fyodorovna to spend the season in the country at her brother's estate.

There, without his work, Ivan Ilyich felt, for the first time, not only boredom but unbearable anguish, and decided that it was impossible to go on like this—that it was necessary to take drastic measures.

After spending a sleepless night pacing the terrace, Ivan Ilyich decided to go to Petersburg and plead his case; in order to punish them—those who had failed to appreciate his worth—he would ask to be transferred to another ministry.

The next day, despite his wife and brother-in-law's best efforts to dissuade him, he set off for Petersburg.

He had only one goal in mind: to secure a post with a salary of 5,000 roubles. He no longer had any preference with regard to any particular ministry, any particular assignment or any particular field of activity. All he needed was a post, a post with a salary of 5,000 roubles, be it in administration, in the banks, with the railways, with the Institutions of the Empress Maria,[6] or even in the customs—but it absolutely must carry a salary of 5,000, and he absolutely must be transferred from the ministry where they had failed to appreciate his worth.

And it so happened that this trip of Ivan Ilyich's was crowned with astonishing, unexpected success. At Kursk his acquaintance F.S. Ilyin entered the first-class carriage and told him that the governor of Kursk had just received a telegram with news concerning the ministry. Great changes were afoot: in a matter of days, Ivan Semyonovich would be named to replace Pyotr Ivanovich.

The prospective change, apart from its significance for Russia, had a special significance for Ivan Ilyich; by bringing forward a new man, Pyotr Petrovich, and, one could assume, his friend Zakhar Ivanovich, it was highly favourable for Ivan Ilyich, who was a colleague and friend of the latter.

In Moscow the news was confirmed, and when Ivan Ilyich arrived in Petersburg, he found Zakhar Ivanovich and was given a promise of a proper post in his former Ministry of Justice.

A week later he telegraphed his wife: "*Zakhar in Miller's place I get appointment at first report.*"

Thanks to this change in personnel, Ivan Ilyich unexpectedly received an appointment in his former ministry that placed him two levels above his colleagues, with a salary of 5,000 roubles plus 3,500 for relocation expenses. All the resentment towards his former enemies and the whole ministry was forgotten. Ivan Ilyich was entirely happy.

He returned to the country more cheerful and satisfied than he had been for a long time. The news had also cheered Praskovya Fyodorovna, and the two of them established a truce. Ivan Ilyich told her of how everyone had fêted him in Petersburg, how all his former enemies had been humiliated and now grovelled before him, how they envied his position and, in particular, how very fond everyone in Petersburg was of him.

Praskovya Fyodorovna listened to all of this and gave the impression of believing it; she didn't contradict a thing, and only made plans for their new life in the town to which they were going. And Ivan Ilyich was delighted to see that her plans were his plans, that he and she were thinking alike, and that his life, which had hit a snag, was once again taking on its natural, authentic character of cheerful pleasantness and decency.

Ivan Ilyich had only returned for a short time. He would have to take up his new duties on 10th September and, of course, he needed time to settle into the new place, to move his possessions from the provinces, to buy and order a great many other things; in a word, to realize the plans he had made in his mind, which corresponded almost exactly to those Praskovya Fyodorovna had made in her heart.

And now that everything had come together so fortuitously, now that he and his wife were working towards the same aim and, moreover, were spending so little time with each other, they achieved a degree of harmony that they had not enjoyed since the first years of their married life. Ivan Ilyich had thought of taking his family with him at once, but the insistence of his wife's brother and sister-in-law, who had suddenly begun to treat him and his family with special warmth and tenderness, persuaded him to go alone.

Ivan Ilyich left, and the cheerful mood brought about by his success and his agreement with his wife, the one reinforcing the other, never abandoned him. He found a lovely apartment, the very thing both husband and wife had been dreaming of. Spacious, with high ceilings, reception rooms in the old style, a grand, commodious study, rooms for wife and daughter, a classroom for the son—it was as if the place had been designed just for them. Ivan Ilyich oversaw the decorating himself, choosing the wallpaper, supplementing the furniture—favouring antiques, which he would have upholstered for an especially *comme il faut* look. Everything grew and grew, gradually approaching his ideal. By the time he was halfway through, the decor had surpassed his expectations. He perceived the *comme il faut*, refined, not at all vulgar character the apartment would take on when it was finished. Drifting into sleep, he would imagine the main reception room in its future form. Looking at the drawing room, he could see the fireplace, the screen, the whatnot, all those little chairs scattered about, the plates and dishes on the walls, the bronzes, as if everything were already in place. He was pleased at the thought of surprising Pasha and Lizanka, who also had a taste for such things. Surely neither of them was expecting this. He had been particularly lucky to find and acquire, rather cheaply, antiques that lent everything an especially noble character. In his letters, he presented the situation as being worse than it was, just so that he could surprise them. All this proved so engrossing that even his new duties, though he liked his work very much indeed, occupied him less than he had expected. On occasion, during sessions, his mind would wander: what sort of cornices should he have for the curtains, straight or curved? He was so engrossed, in fact, that he often took matters into his own hands, rearranging the furniture and rehanging the curtains. One time, when climbing a ladder in order to show the upholsterer, who had failed to understand, exactly how he wanted the curtains draped, he lost his footing and fell, but being a strong and agile man, he managed to hold on and only knocked his side against the knob on the window frame. The bruise was painful, but the pain soon passed. Throughout it all, Ivan Ilyich felt especially cheerful and healthy. He wrote: "I feel like I've dropped fifteen years off my age." The plan had been to finish in September, but the process dragged on until the middle of October. The result was worth waiting for: utterly charming—and not only in his view, but also according to every person who laid eyes on it.

In essence, of course, what one saw was what one always sees in the homes of not quite rich people who make an effort to appear rich and, in so doing, only come to look like one another: damasks, ebony, flowers, carpets and bronzes—every dark and lustrous thing that all people of a certain kind procure in order to look like all people of a certain kind. Indeed, his home looked so much like every home of its sort that it wouldn't attract the least bit of attention; to him, however, it all seemed to be quite exceptional.

It was a joy for him to meet his family at the railway station and bring them to his brightly lit, finished apartment, where a footman in a white tie opened the door into a front hall decked with flowers—a joy to lead them into the drawing room, the study, everywhere, and a joy to hear their gasps of pleasure at each step. He himself beamed with pleasure as he drank in their praise. That same evening, when Praskovya Fyodorovna asked him incidentally, over tea, about his fall, he laughed and demonstrated how he had gone flying and frightened the upholsterer.

"A good thing I'm a gymnast. A lesser man might have killed himself—I just got a knock here. Hurts a bit when you touch it, but getting better already. Just a bruise."

So they began their life in their new home—finding, as always, once they settled in, that they were just one room shy of comfort—on their new income, which was, as always, a little shy (by some five hundred roubles) of what they needed, and all was going very nicely indeed. It went especially nicely at first, before everything was arranged, when certain things still needed doing: this to buy, that to order, this to move, that to adjust. There were, to be sure, some disagreements between husband and wife, but both were so satisfied and so busy that major quarrels were avoided. It was only when all the arrangements had been made that a degree of boredom set in, that they began to feel something was lacking—but then they struck up new acquaintances, developed new habits, and life became full again.

After a morning spent in court, Ivan Ilyich would return for dinner, and at first his mood was good, though it did suffer slightly on account of the house. (Every stain on the tablecloth or damask, every torn curtain sash irritated him: he had put so much work into arranging things that the slightest deterioration caused him pain.) But, in general, Ivan Ilyich's life progressed as he believed life should progress: easily, pleasantly and decently. Every morning he got up at nine, drank his coffee, read his paper, then put on his uniform and set out for court. The harness in which he worked had already been stretched to fit him comfortably, and he would slip into it without delay. The petitioners, the inquiries in the chancery, the chancery itself and the sessions, both public and administrative—the key in every instance was to exclude all that was raw and vital, which invariably interrupted the orderly flow of official business. No unofficial relations were to be permitted; one must only have relations with people on official grounds, in official terms. For example, a man comes in with a question. Ivan Ilyich, in his unofficial capacity, can have no relations with such a man. But if this man had some relation to Ivan Ilyich in the latter's role as a member of the court, some relation that could be expressed on official headed paper, then Ivan Ilyich would do everything, absolutely everything possible within the limits of said relation, all the while maintaining the semblance of friendly human relations, that is, of common courtesy. As soon as the official relation is ended, so too end all others. Ivan Ilyich possessed this ability to separate his official business from his real life in the highest degree— and by long practice and natural talent he managed to refine it to such a point that, on occasion, he would even allow himself, like a playful virtuoso, to blend human and official relations. He allowed himself to do this because he felt sure of his power to single out the official side of things at any point he needed, casting aside the human. And he managed this feat not only easily, pleasantly and decently, but with virtuosic grace. During the intervals between sessions he smoked, drank tea, chatted a bit about politics, a bit about general topics of the day, a bit about cards and, most of all, about official appointments. Then, tired, but with the feeling of a virtuoso, of a first violin who has performed his part masterfully, he would return home. And there he would find that his wife and daughter had been out, or had had guests, that his son had gone to school and was now doing his homework with his tutors, diligently studying whatever it was they taught boys his age. Everything was in order, all was well. After dinner, if there were no visitors, Ivan Ilyich might read a book people were talking about, and later in the evening he would settle down to work—that is, pore over documents, comparing depositions and squaring them with the statutes. He found this work neither boring nor amusing. It was boring when he could instead be playing bridge, but if bridge wasn't an option, it was still better than idling away the hours alone or with his wife. The true pleasure of Ivan Ilyich's life lay in hosting little dinners, to which he invited ladies and gentlemen of high social standing; he passed his time with them in much the same way as people of their sort generally passed their time, just as his drawing room was much the same as all other drawing rooms.

One time they even gave a dance. Ivan Ilyich had a merry time, and all went swimmingly, but it did lead to an awful quarrel with his wife, over the cakes and sweets. Praskovya Fyodorovna had it all planned out, but Ivan Ilyich insisted on buying everything from an expensive confectioner. He bought quite a lot of cakes and the quarrel broke out because many of these were left untouched, while the confectioner's bill ran to forty-five roubles. It was a big, nasty quarrel and Praskovya Fyodorovna ended up calling him a "sour old fool", at which point he lost his temper, clutched his head with both hands and said something about divorce. But the dance itself was a merry affair. The finest people had come and Ivan Ilyich took a few turns with Princess Trufonova, whose sister had famously established the Society "Bear My Grief to Distant Shores".[7] The joy Ivan Ilyich derived from work was a matter of ambition; the joy he derived from social occasions was a matter of vanity; his true joy lay in bridge. He readily admitted that, whatever may come, whatever unpleasantness might befall him in life, the joy that shone like a bright candle, brighter than all others, was to sit down to bridge with good players and soft-spoken partners—four in all (with five it was terribly unpleasant to sit out a hand, though one pretended to enjoy it)—and to play an intelligent, serious game (if the cards were in favour of it), followed by supper and a glass of wine. And after a game of bridge, especially if he had won a little (to win too large a sum is unseemly), Ivan Ilyich always went to bed in a particularly good mood.

Such was their life. Their social circle was of the finest sort; they were visited by significant people, and by the young.

Husband, wife and daughter were unanimous in their view of their social set and, without coordinating their efforts, systematically rid themselves of all sorts of bedraggled friends and relatives who flocked, full of tender endearments, into their drawing room, with its Japanese plates on the walls. Before long these bedraggled friends no longer came flocking and the Golovins were surrounded by only the best people. Young men came to call on Lizanka. Petrishchev, an examining magistrate and sole heir to his father Dmitry Ivanovich Petrishchev's estate, had begun to court her, and Ivan Ilyich had already spoken with Praskovya Fyodorovna about arranging a sleigh ride for the pair, or perhaps a little performance. Such was their life. On it went, without change, and all was well.

IV

All were in good health. It could not be said that Ivan Ilyich was in poor health just because he sometimes complained of an odd taste in his mouth or felt discomfort in the left side of his stomach.

But then that discomfort began to increase, transforming not quite into pain, but into a constant feeling of heaviness in his side, accompanied by a bad mood. And this bad mood, growing worse and worse, began to spoil the pleasantly easy and decorous way of life that had all but established itself in the Golovin household. As husband and wife began to quarrel more and more frequently, the ease and pleasantness soon fell away; that left only decorum, and it too was hanging on by a thread. Scenes, once again, became a common occurrence. Once again, there remained only islets on which husband and wife could meet without an explosion, and these islets were few and far between.

Now Praskovya Fyodorovna could say with some justification that her husband had a bad temper. And being prone as she was to exaggeration, she claimed that his temper had always been this dreadful and that it had needed all her kindness to endure it these past twenty years. It was true that he now instigated the quarrels. The nagging always commenced right before dinner, and often just as he began to eat, over soup. He might find some flaw in the plates or dishes, or the meal might fail to please him, or he might not like that his son had put an elbow on the table or the way his daughter had done up her hair.

In his eyes, Praskovya Fyodorovna was invariably to blame. When this had first started, she would object and say unpleasant things to him, but on a couple of occasions he had flown into such a rage at the beginning of dinner that she realized the cause was a painful reaction to the intake of food, and so she began to restrain herself; she no longer objected, only hurried to get through the meal. Praskovya Fyodorovna took great pride in her self-restraint. Having decided once and for all that her husband had a dreadful temper and, indeed, that he had brought about her life's misfortune, she began to pity herself. And the more she pitied herself, the more she came to despise her husband. She began to wish him dead, but she could not really wish that, because it would mean the end of his salary. And this only fed her irritation against him. She considered herself terribly unfortunate precisely because even her husband's death could not save her; and so she was irritated, concealed it, and her concealed irritation intensified his irritation.

After one scene during which Ivan Ilyich had been especially unfair and after which, in an attempt to explain himself, he had admitted that he was indeed irritable, but that this was due to illness, Praskovya Fyodorovna said that if he was ill, then he had to seek treatment, and demanded that he go and see a well-known physician.

He went. It was all exactly as he had expected it would be, exactly as it always is. There was the wait, the physician's affected air of importance—so familiar to him, since he affected that very same air in court—the tapping and auscultation, the questions that called for prepared and evidently unnecessary answers, and an appearance of significance that suggested, *You just submit yourself to us and we'll arrange everything; we know full well, without a shadow of a doubt, how to arrange everything, for it is always the same, for every person.* It was all exactly as it is in court. The well-known doctor affected the same air in his presence as he himself affected when looking down at the accused.

The doctor said: *So-and-so indicates that inside of you there is such-and-such; but if it is not confirmed by an analysis of this-and-that, then we must assume you have such-and-such. If we assume such-and-such, then...* and so on. For Ivan Ilyich, only one question mattered: was his condition dangerous or not? But the doctor ignored this inappropriate question. From the doctor's point of view it was an idle question, not worth considering; the problem at hand was to weigh the probabilities of a floating kidney, chronic catarrh or a disease of the blind gut. This was not a question of Ivan Ilyich's life and death, it was a dispute between a floating kidney and the blind gut. And right before Ivan Ilyich's eyes, the doctor resolved this dispute quite brilliantly in favour of the blind gut, with the reservation that should the urine analysis provide new evidence the case would be reviewed. All this was precisely what Ivan Ilyich had himself done a thousand times, in just as brilliant a manner, when looking down at the accused. The doctor was also brilliant in summing up the case, glancing triumphantly, even cheerfully, over his spectacles at the accused. The summing-up led Ivan Ilyich to the conclusion that things looked bad—the doctor and, perhaps, everyone else—couldn't be bothered, but for him things looked bad. And this conclusion came as a painful blow, arousing in him a feeling of great self-pity as well as of great anger towards this doctor, who was wholly indifferent to so important a question.

But he kept this to himself, rose, put money on the table and said with a sigh: "We patients probably often pose inappropriate questions. But I would like to know, is this illness dangerous or not?"

The doctor gave him a stern one-eyed glance through his spectacles, as if to say: *If the accused refuses to stay within the bounds of the questions posed to him, I will be compelled to order him removed from the court.*

"I have already told you what I consider necessary and expedient. The results of the analysis will tell us more." And the doctor bowed.

Ivan Ilyich went out slowly, seated himself mournfully in his sleigh and drove home. He spent the entire journey going over all that the doctor had said, trying to translate all those tangled, obscure, scientific words into plain speech and to make out in them an answer to the question: *Is it bad—is it very bad, or is there still nothing to worry about?* And it seemed to him that the burden of what the doctor had said was that things were very bad. Everything in the streets looked bleak to Ivan Ilyich. The cabmen and the houses, the passers-by and the shops—they were all bleak. And the pain, the dull, aching pain that never ceased for a moment, seemed to acquire a new, more serious meaning in connection with the doctor's obscure words. Ivan Ilyich now monitored it closely with a new, oppressive feeling.

At home he began to tell his wife what had happened. She listened, but in the middle of his story their daughter came into the room with a hat on: the two women had been preparing to go out. The daughter took a seat and made an effort to listen to all this dreary talk, but she could not stand it long and her mother did not let him finish.

"Well, that's all very good to hear," she said. "Now you'll just have to make sure to take your medicine on time. Give me the prescription and I'll send Gerasim to the chemist's." With that she went out to get dressed.

He had hardly paused for breath while she was in the room, and now that she was gone he heaved a deep sigh.

"Well, then," he said. "Maybe it really is nothing…"

He began to take his medicine and to follow the doctor's instructions, which had changed in light of the urine analysis. But here there was some confusion, a contradiction between the results of the analysis and what was supposed to follow from these results. It was impossible to reach the doctor himself, but what Ivan Ilyich was experiencing was not what the doctor had told him he would experience. The doctor had either forgotten, or lied, or was concealing something from him.

Nevertheless, Ivan Ilyich began to follow his instructions in every detail and at first found comfort in doing so.

After his visit to the doctor, Ivan Ilyich's primary occupation became the exact execution of the doctor's instructions regarding hygiene and the taking of medicine, as well as the monitoring of his pain and of all his bodily functions. Ivan Ilyich's primary interests were now human illnesses and human health. Whenever he heard mention of someone falling ill, or dying, or recovering—especially when it concerned a disease similar to his own—he would listen closely, trying to conceal his agitation and would ask many questions, applying all that he heard to himself.

Ivan Ilyich's pain did not decrease, but he made an effort to force himself to think that he was better. And he would manage to deceive himself, so long as nothing unnerved him. But as soon as he faced any sort of unpleasantness with his wife, difficulty at work or a run of bad cards at bridge, his illness would make itself felt in full force. In the past he could withstand such difficulties, remaining confident in his power to set things right, win the day, attain success, make a grand slam—but now they knocked him off his feet and plunged him into despair. He would say to himself: *Just as I was starting to recover, just when the medicine was taking effect, this damned reversal...* And he grew angry at the misfortune or at the people who were causing him trouble, who were killing him, and he could feel that the anger itself was killing him but he could not restrain it. It seems it should have been clear to him that his exasperation at circumstances and people aggravated his illness, and that he should therefore ignore all these unpleasant incidents, but his mind came to a wholly different conclusion: he said he needed peace, kept a close eye on anything that might disturb that peace and grew irritated at the slightest disturbance. His situation was made worse by the fact that he read medical books and consulted doctors. The deterioration of his condition was so gradual that he could deceive himself by comparing one day to another—there was hardly any difference. But when he consulted doctors, it seemed to him that he was indeed getting worse, and rather quickly too. Yet he consulted them constantly.

That month he visited another celebrity who told him almost the same thing as the first celebrity but put his questions differently. The consultation with this second celebrity only worsened Ivan Ilyich's doubts and fears. A friend of a friend—a very fine doctor—determined his illness to be something else entirely, and although he promised a full recovery, his questions and assumptions confused Ivan Ilyich still further and increased his doubts. A homeopath made another diagnosis and offered medicine that Ivan Ilyich took for a full week, in secret. But when the week had passed, Ivan Ilyich felt no relief. He lost faith both in this and in all his previous treatments, sinking deeper in despair. One time a lady acquaintance of his was saying something about healing with the aid of icons. Ivan Ilyich caught himself listening attentively and coming to believe in the reality of this phenomenon. The incident frightened him. *Has my mind really gone this soft?* he asked himself. *Absolute nonsense! No, I won't give in to anxiety—I must choose one doctor and follow his course of treatment to the end. That's exactly what I'll do. No more of this. I won't think about it—I'll simply follow one course of treatment until the summer. Then we'll see. For now, no more dithering!* This was easy to say but impossible to do. The pain in his side was agonizing; it seemed to grow worse and worse, becoming constant. The taste in his mouth became ever more strange and it seemed to him that his breath stank of something awful. He was losing his appetite and his strength. He could no longer deceive himself: something terrifying, new and more significant than anything Ivan Ilyich had ever experienced in his whole life was transpiring within him. And he alone knew it. Everyone around him either did not understand or did not wish to understand, believing that all was going on as usual. This was what tormented Ivan Ilyich most. He saw that the members of his household—especially his wife and daughter, who were in the very midst of the busiest social season—understood nothing and were annoyed that he was so dispirited and demanding, as if this were his fault. Although they tried to hide it, he saw that he was a nuisance to them but that his wife had developed a definite attitude towards his illness and maintained it regardless of what he said or did. That attitude was the following:

"You know," she would say to acquaintances, "Ivan Ilyich simply can't do as decent people do and follow the course of treatment prescribed to him. Today he might take his drops, eat what he's told to eat, and go to bed in good time. But the next day, if I take my eyes off him for a moment, he'll forget to take his drops, will eat sturgeon—strictly forbidden—and will stay up playing cards till one o'clock in the morning."

"Oh, come now, how often has that happened?" Ivan Ilyich would ask, rather chagrined. "Just that one time at Pyotr Ivanovich's."

"And last night with Shebek."

"I couldn't sleep anyway, because of the pain."

"Excuses, excuses… The point is you'll never get better this way and will go on tormenting us."

Praskovya Fyodorovna's external attitude towards her husband's illness, which she expressed both to others and to Ivan Ilyich, was that her husband had only himself to blame, and that it was merely a new source of trouble for his wife. Ivan Ilyich felt that these thoughts escaped her involuntarily, but that did not make things any easier for him.

And in court Ivan Ilyich also noticed, or thought he noticed, a strange attitude towards himself: sometimes he sensed he was being watched as a person who was soon to vacate his place; and then, all of a sudden, his closest colleagues might begin to poke good-natured fun at his hypochondria, as if that awful, frightening, unheard-of entity that had lodged itself inside him—that was incessantly gnawing away at him, irresistibly dragging him off towards some unknown fate—was the most pleasant subject for a joke. Ivan Ilyich was especially irritated by Schwartz, whose playfulness, vitality and unfaltering *savoir faire* reminded him of himself ten years before.

His friends come for a game and sit down to play. They deal the cards, breaking in a new deck. He finds he has seven diamonds. His partner says "no trumps" and supports him with two diamonds. What else could he possibly want? He has every reason to be cheerful—a grand slam. But then comes that gnawing pain, that taste in his mouth, and it begins to seem absurd that he should find pleasure in a grand slam under these circumstances.

He watches Mikhail Mikhaylovich, his partner, who raps the table with a ruddy hand and politely, condescendingly refrains from gathering up the tricks, instead nudging them towards Ivan Ilyich, so as to give him the pleasure of collecting them without having to stretch out his hand. *What, does he think me too weak to stretch out my hand?* Ivan Ilyich wonders, forgetting the trumps and over-trumping his own, thereby losing the grand slam by three tricks. And the most dreadful part is that he sees how all this upsets Mikhail Mikhaylovich, but to him none of it matters. And it is horrifying to consider why none of it matters.

They all see that he is struggling and so they tell him: "We don't have to go on if you're tired. You need your rest." Rest? No, he is not at all tired and they finish the rubber. All are gloomy and silent. Ivan Ilyich feels that it is he who has cast this gloom over them and he cannot dispel it. They dine and depart, and Ivan Ilyich remains alone with the knowledge that his life has been poisoned and now poisons the lives of others, and that this poison does not weaken but penetrates ever deeper, permeating his entire being.

And with this knowledge, as well as the physical pain, as well as the horror, he had to go to bed and, frequently, lie awake, suffering, most of the night. The next morning he would have to rise again, dress, go to court, speak, write—or, perhaps, stay at home in the company of the same twenty-four hours of the day, every last one of which was torture. And he was forced to live this way, on the brink of annihilation, all alone, with not a single person to understand and pity him.

V

So one month passed, then another. Just before the New Year his brother-in-law came to town and stayed at their place. Ivan Ilyich was in court when he arrived and Praskovya Fyodorovna was out shopping. When Ivan Ilyich returned and entered his study, he found his brother-in-law—a healthy, sanguine fellow—unpacking his suitcase by himself. He raised his head at the sound of Ivan Ilyich's footsteps and, for a moment, gazed at him in silence. For Ivan Ilyich, this gaze revealed everything. His brother-in-law opened his mouth and nearly gasped, but checked himself in time. That confirmed it.

"I've changed, yes?"

"Yes... there is a change."

And after that, no matter how much Ivan Ilyich tried to turn the conversation back to the matter of his physical appearance, his brother-in-law refused to say more. Praskovya Fyodorovna returned and the brother-in-law went out to greet her. Ivan Ilyich locked the door and began to examine himself in the mirror, first from the front, then from the side. He picked up a photograph of himself with Praskovya Fyodorovna and began to compare the portrait with what he saw in the mirror. The change was immense. Then he bared his arms up to the elbow, took a look, pulled his sleeves down again, lowered himself onto the ottoman and grew blacker than the night.

*No, you mustn't let yourself. . .* he thought, jumped up, went to the table, opened a brief and tried to read it—but he could not. He unlocked the door and went into the reception room. The door to the drawing room was closed. He sneaked up to it on tiptoe and listened.

"No, you're exaggerating," Praskovya Fyodorovna was saying.

"Exaggerating? Can't you see? He's a dead man. . . Just look at his eyes—the light's gone. What is it that he's got, exactly?"

"No one knows. Nikolayev (this was another doctor) said something, but I don't know. Leshchetitsky (the well-known doctor) doesn't agree. . ."

Ivan Ilyich stepped away from the door, walked to his room, lay down and began to think: *A kidney. A floating kidney.* He remembered everything that the doctors had told him—how the kidney had come loose, how it was floating about. And by an effort of imagination he tried to catch this kidney, to stop it and fasten it in place; it seemed so little was needed to do so, *No, I'll go to see Pyotr Ivanovich.* (This was the friend who was friends with the doctor.) He rang, ordered his sleigh and got ready to go.

"Jean, where are you going?" his wife asked in an especially mournful and unusually kind manner.

This unusual kindness exasperated him. He looked at her sullenly.

"I must go to Pyotr Ivanovich's."

He went to see his friend who was friends with the doctor. Then they both went to see the doctor. The doctor was in and he had a long consultation with Ivan Ilyich.

Going over the anatomical and physiological details of what, according to the doctor, was occurring within him, he understood everything.

There was one little thing, a tiny thing, in his blind gut. It could all be set right. If he were to stimulate the energy of one organ and weaken the activity of another, absorption would occur and all would be set right. He was a bit late for dinner. He ate, spoke gaily, but for a long time could not force himself back to his desk. At last he went off to his study and busied himself. He read briefs, did his work, but he could not rid himself of the sense that he was deferring an important, intimate matter to which he would return when all else was done. And when he had finished his work he remembered that this intimate matter was the thought of his blind gut. But he did not give in to it and instead went to the drawing room for tea. They had guests, including the examining magistrate whom the daughter wished to marry, and there was much talking, playing the piano, singing. Throughout the evening Ivan Ilyich was, as Praskovya Fyodorovna remarked, more cheerful than anyone, but he did not for a moment forget that he had deferred the important thought of the blind gut. At eleven o'clock he said goodnight and went to his bedroom. He had been sleeping alone since he fell ill, in a small room next to his study. He entered, undressed and took up a novel by Zola, but he did not read it; instead, he gave himself over to thought. In his imagination, the desired correction of the blind gut was taking place—the absorption, the expulsion, the restoration of normal functioning. *Yes, that's the way*, he told himself. *Simply a matter of assisting nature.*

He remembered his medicine, got up, took it and lay down on his back, paying close attention to the medicine's healthful effect, its destruction of pain. *Simply a matter of taking it regularly and avoiding harmful influences. I feel a bit better already, much better.* He began to palpate his abdomen—it was no longer painful to the touch. *I don't feel a thing—yes, much better.* He put out the candle and turned on his side... The blind gut was correcting itself, absorbing. But then he felt it: that old, familiar, dull, gnawing pain—silent, stubborn and serious. And in his mouth he felt that same disgusting taste. His heart sank and his head began to spin. "My God, my God," he muttered. "Again, again—and it will never stop." And suddenly the question presented itself quite differently. *Blind gut! Kidney,* he told himself. *This isn't a matter of the blind gut or kidney, it's a matter of life and... death. Yes, I had life in me, and now it is leaving, leaving, and I cannot hold on to it. Yes. Why deceive myself? Is it not obvious to all but me that I am dying? That it's only a question of weeks, of days—maybe now? There was light and now there is darkness. I was here and now I am there... Where?* An icy coldness swept over him and his breath stopped. He heard only the beating of his heart.

*I'll be gone—and what then? Nothing. So where will I go, where will I be? Is this... is this death? No, no...* He

LEO TOLSTOY

started up in bed, fumbled with trembling hands for the candle, dropped it on the floor and fell back on the pillow. *What's the use? It doesn't matter*, he told himself, staring into the darkness with wide-open eyes. *Death. Yes, death. And not one of them knows it—not one of them wants to know, wants to take pity. They're playing.* (He heard the distant sound of singing with accompaniment from behind the door.) *They don't care—but they'll die too. The fools. I'll die before them, but they too will die, they'll die all the same. And listen to them enjoying themselves… Beasts.* He choked with malice and felt crushed by a terrible, unbearable weight. Is it possible that everyone was doomed to suffer this dreadful horror? He sat up.

*No, something's not right. I must calm down, think things over from the beginning.* And he began thinking. *Yes, the start of my illness. I bumped my side and not much changed, that day and the next; it ached a little, then a bit more, then the doctors, dejection, depression, more doctors… And the whole time I was getting closer, closer to the abyss. Losing my strength… Getting closer, closer… And here I am, wasted away. The light is gone from my eyes. And this is death—but I'm thinking about my gut. I'm thinking about repairing my gut—but this is death. Is it? Is it really death?* And again he was seized with horror. Gasping for breath, he bent down and began to hunt for matches, pressing his elbow against the nightstand. The nightstand was in his way; it hurt him. He grew annoyed with it, angry, and pressed against it more forcefully, knocking it over. Panting in despair, he fell on his back, expecting death to come at once.

The guests were leaving then and Praskovya Fyodorovna was seeing them off. She heard the thud and entered his room.

"What's the matter?"

"Nothing. It was an accident."

She went out and brought in a candle. He lay there, breathing heavily, rapidly, like a man who had run a mile, and stared up at her with unmoving eyes.

"Jean, what is it?"

"No…thing. An… acci…dent." (*What sense is there in telling her?* he thought. *She'd never understand.*)

And indeed, she understood nothing. She picked up the nightstand, lit his candle and hurried away to see another guest off.

When she returned he was in the same position, lying on his back, staring up.

"What's the matter? Are you feeling worse?"

"Yes."

She shook her head and sat down next to him.

"You know, Jean, I think we should ask Leshchetitsky to come and see you."

This meant that they should call in a well-known doctor, never mind the cost. He gave her a venomous smile and said: "No." She sat a while longer, then went over and kissed him on the forehead.

He hated her with every fibre of his being as she kissed him and had to force himself not to push her away.

"Good night. God willing, you'll get some sleep."

"Yes."

VI

Ivan Ilyich saw that he was dying, and he was in constant despair.

Deep down, Ivan Ilyich knew that he was dying, but he not only failed to accustom himself to this fact, he simply did not and could not understand it.

That syllogism he had studied in Kiesewetter's *Logic*[8]—"Caius is a man, men are mortal, therefore Caius is mortal"—had seemed to him throughout his whole life to be correct only in relation to Caius, but certainly not to himself. That was the case for *the man Caius*, man in the abstract, and it was perfectly just—but he himself was not Caius, not man in the abstract. He had always been an entirely unique being, quite separate from all others; he was Vanya—Vanya with his mama, his papa, with Mitya and Volodya, with his toys, the coachman, his nanny and then with Katenka, with all the joys, griefs and raptures of childhood, boyhood and youth. What had Caius to do with the smell of that striped leather ball which Vanya had loved so much? Was it Caius who had kissed Mother's hand like that, and had the silk of her dress rustled in that special way for Caius? Had Caius led the charge for better pastries in law school? Did Caius fall so deeply in love? Was Caius capable of presiding over a session with such dignity?

*Yes, Caius is definitely mortal, and it's right that he should die, but me, Vanya, Ivan Ilyich, with all my feelings, my thoughts—no, with me it's different. It is impossible that I should die. That would be too horrible.*

That was how he felt.

*If I were meant to die like Caius, then I would have known it—my inner voice would have told me so. But I sensed nothing, nothing of the sort. All my friends and I, we understood that with us things stood differently, that we were not like Caius. And now this,* he thought. *No, it can't be. It can't—but it is. How? How am I to understand it?*

Indeed he could not understand it and so he tried to reject the thought as false, incorrect, unhealthy, and to supplant it with different, correct, healthy thoughts. Yet the thought—and not only the thought, it seemed, but the reality of it—kept returning again and again to confront him.

And in place of the thought he would call up a series of other thoughts, seeking in them a crutch. He tried to revert to his old ways of thinking, which had previously obscured the thought of death. But, strangely enough, all that had previously obscured, concealed, destroyed his awareness of death no longer had the power to do so. In recent days, Ivan Ilyich spent most of his time attempting to restore those old modes of feeling that had once obscured death. He would say to himself: *I'll go back to work. After all, I used to live by it.* And so, dismissing all doubts, he would go to court. There he would engage his colleagues in conversation, take his seat and survey the crowd in his customary manner, absentminded, meditative, leaning both his emaciated arms on the arms of the oaken chair; as usual, he would bend towards his colleague, draw his papers nearer and exchange whispers, then, suddenly raising his eyes and sitting up straight, he would pronounce those well-known words and open the proceedings. But then, midway through the session, with no regard for the stage the proceedings had reached, the pain in his side would proceed with *its own* gnawing work.

Ivan Ilyich would attend to the pain, would try to banish the thought of it, but the pain would go on about its work and *it* would return to confront him, staring straight at him—and he would be petrified, the spark would die out from his eyes and he would again ask himself: *Can it really be the only truth?* And his colleagues and subordinates would look on with surprise and dismay as he, a brilliant, subtle judge, grew confused and made mistakes. He would shake himself, try to come to his senses and would somehow bring the session to a close. And then he would return home, depressingly aware that his judicial work could no longer conceal from him, as it had always done before, what he so wished to conceal; his judicial work could not rid him of *it*. And worst of all, *it* drew his attention towards itself not so that he might do something about it, but only that he should look at it, stare straight into its eyes—that he should look at it, do nothing and suffer unspeakably.

To protect himself from this suffering, Ivan Ilyich looked for solace, for other screens; such screens were found and, for a short time, seemed to protect him, but all at once they would not so much crumble as turn transparent, as if *it* were able to penetrate anything and nothing could obscure *it*.

At times, of late, he would go into the drawing room he had decorated—the drawing room where he had fallen and for the sake of which (how bitterly absurd it now seemed) he had sacrificed his life, for he knew that his illness had begun with that bruise—he would go in and spot, say, a scratch on the lacquered table. He would search for the cause of the scratch and find it in the bronze ornamentation of an album, the edge of which had been bent. He would take up the expensive album, which he had compiled with love and care, and grow irritated at the negligence of his daughter and her friends—pages torn, photographs turned upside down. He would diligently set things right, bending the ornamentation back into place.

Then it would occur to him that the entire *établissement* with the albums ought to be placed in another corner, where the flowers were. He would call the footman, but cither his wife or daughter could come to help; they would disagree with him, contradict him and he would argue, grow angry—yet all was well because *it* was forgotten, *it* was out of sight.

But then, as he was moving something himself, his wife would say: "Let the servants do it. You'll just hurt yourself again." And suddenly *it* would flash through the screen. He would catch sight of *it*—just a flash, so there was still hope that *it* might disappear, but, despite himself, he would turn his attention to his side: and there the thing was, gnawing away. And now he could no longer forget; now *it* was clearly staring at him from behind the flowers. Why bother at all?

*Is it true? Did I really lose my life here, on this curtain, as at the storming of some fort? How terrible and how foolish… No, it can't be true, it can't… But it is.*

He would go to his study, lie down and again be alone with *it*—face to face with *it*. And there was nothing to do with *it* but to look at *it* and grow cold.

VII

How this came about it was impossible to say, because it happened step by step, imperceptibly, but what happened was this: in the third month of Ivan Ilyich's illness, his wife, his daughter, his son, his servants, his acquaintances, his doctors and, most importantly, he himself became aware that the only thing about him that was of interest to others was whether he would soon, at long last, vacate his place, liberate the living from the embarrassment caused by his presence and be himself liberated from his sufferings.

He slept less and less. He was given opium and, later, injections of morphine, but this did not relieve him. The dull depression he would experience in a state of half-sleep at first only brought him relief as something new, but then it became just as excruciating as the undisguised pain, perhaps even more so.

Special foods were prepared for him on doctors' orders, but he found these foods ever more tasteless, ever more disgusting.

Special arrangements were also made for his evacuations and this proved a torment every time—a torment due to the filth, the indecency and the smell, and due to the consciousness that another person had to take part in it.

Yet it was through this most unpleasant affair that Ivan Ilyich found a degree of comfort. Gerasim, the butler's helper, always came in to take the things away.

Gerasim was a clean, fresh peasant lad, grown stout on town fare—always cheerful, always bright. At first the sight of this fellow in his clean peasant garb performing that nasty task perturbed Ivan Ilyich.

One time he rose from the vessel and, too weak to lift up his trousers, collapsed into a soft armchair and stared with horror at his naked, feeble thighs, their muscles standing out in such sharp relief.

Gerasim walked in with light, firm steps, filling the room with the pleasant scent of the tar from his thick boots and of fresh winter air, wearing a clean hempen apron and a clean cotton shirt, with its sleeves rolled up over his strong young forearms; and without looking at Ivan Ilyich—evidently holding back the joy of life that shone on his face, so as not to offend the sick man—he approached the vessel.

"Gerasim," Ivan Ilyich called out in a weak voice.

Gerasim winced, evidently afraid that he had made some sort of mistake, and with a quick movement turned his fresh, kind, simple young face, which was just beginning to sprout whiskers, towards the sick man.

"Yes, sir?"

"This must be very unpleasant for you. I'm sorry. I have no choice."

"For goodness' sake, sir." Gerasim's eyes sparkled and he bared his young white teeth. "Why shouldn't I do a little work? You've got a case of sickness."

With deft, strong hands he performed his usual task and went out, stepping lightly. Five minutes later, stepping just as lightly, he returned.

Ivan Ilyich had not moved from the armchair.

"Gerasim," he said, after the lad had set down the freshly washed vessel. "Please come here, help me." Gerasim approached. "Lift me up. It's hard for me to do it by myself, and I've sent Dmitry away."

Gerasim came closer to Ivan Ilyich and, just as lightly as he stepped, embraced him with his strong hands and lifted him with a deft, gentle movement; he held him upright with one hand, pulled up his trousers with the other, and was about to sit him down, but Ivan Ilyich asked to be led to the sofa. Effortlessly, without applying, it seemed, any pressure at all, Gerasim led him—almost carried him—to the sofa and sat him down.

"Thank you. You… you do everything so deftly, so well."

Gerasim smiled again and was about to leave. But Ivan Ilyich felt so good in the lad's presence that he did not wish to let him go.

"Listen, would you bring that chair closer, please? No, that other one there. Put it under my feet. I feel better when my feet are up."

Gerasim brought the chair, set it down firmly without making a noise and lifted Ivan Ilyich's legs onto the seat. It seemed to Ivan Ilyich that he felt better while Gerasim was holding his legs.

"It's better when my feet are higher," he said. "Lay that cushion under them."

Gerasim did as he was asked. He lifted Ivan

Ilyich's legs and set them down. Once again, Ivan Ilyich felt better as long as Gerasim was holding his legs; when Gerasim lowered them, he seemed to feel worse.

"Gerasim," he said. "Are you busy now?"

"Not at all, sir," replied Gerasim, who had learnt from the townspeople how to speak to gentlefolk.

"What else have you got to do today?"

"Not a thing, really—did it all, aside from chopping the firewood."

"Well, then, could you hold my legs higher?"

"Sure can." Gerasim raised his master's legs—and it seemed to Ivan Ilyich that, in this position, he felt no pain at all.

"What about the firewood?"

"Don't you worry about that. Plenty of time."

Ivan Ilyich told Gerasim to sit down and hold his legs. He and the lad had a talk. And, strangely enough, it seemed to him he felt better while Gerasim was holding his legs.

After that Ivan Ilyich would sometimes call Gerasim and make him hold his legs on his shoulders, happily chatting with the lad. Gerasim did this easily, willingly, simply and with a kindness that touched his master. Ivan Ilyich was offended by the health, strength and vitality of all others, but the strength and vitality of Gerasim did not upset him—it soothed him.

Ivan Ilyich's greatest torment was the lie—a lie that was, for some reason, accepted by everyone—according to which he was merely ill, not dying, and only had to remain calm, take his treatment and then something very good would result. He knew, of course, that no matter what was done, the only result would be still greater suffering and death. This lie tormented him; he was tormented by the fact that no one was willing to admit what everyone knew and what he himself knew, that they instead wished to lie about his dreadful situation, and that they wished and forced him to take part in this lie. This lie, a lie spun around him on the eve of his death—a lie that forcibly brought the terrible, solemn act of his death down to the level of all their visits, their curtains, their sturgeon for dinner—was enormously painful for Ivan Ilyich. And strangely enough, on many occasions, when they were performing their little acts around him, he was a hair's breadth away from shouting: *Stop it! I'm dying—you know it and I know it—so at least stop lying about it!* But he could never work up the courage to do it. He saw that everyone around him had relegated the terrible, frightful act of his dying to the level of a casual unpleasantness, a slight indecency (as when someone enters a drawing room and makes a bad smell), and they had done so by virtue of the very "decency" he had served his entire life. He saw that no one would pity him, because no one even wished to understand his situation. Gerasim alone understood it and pitied him. And so Ivan Ilyich felt good only with Gerasim. He felt good when Gerasim held his legs, at times all night long, refusing to go to bed—"Don't you worry, Ivan Ilyich, I'll get my sleep yet"—or when he would suddenly adopt a familiar tone and say, "It'd be one thing if you wasn't sick, but things being what they are, why shouldn't I do a little work?" Gerasim alone did not lie; it was obvious that he alone understood what was happening, felt no need to conceal it and simply pitied his weak, emaciated master. One time, when Ivan Ilyich was sending him away, Gerasim even said straight out: "We'll all be dying someday. So why shouldn't I do a little work?" What he meant by this was that he did not feel burdened by the work he was doing, because he was doing it for a dying man and he hoped someone would do the same for him when his time came.

In addition to this lie, or as a consequence of it, what tormented Ivan Ilyich most was the fact that no one pitied him the way he wished to be pitied. There were times when Ivan Ilyich, after much suffering, wished above all else—however much it shamed him to admit it—to be pitied as sick children are pitied. He wanted someone to kiss, caress and weep over him, as they would caress and console a child. He knew that he was an important member of the court, that his beard had begun to turn grey and that what he desired was therefore impossible—but he still desired it. He found something like it in his relationship with Gerasim, and so this relationship was of great comfort to him. Ivan Ilyich wanted to cry, wanted someone to caress him, to weep over him—but in comes his colleague, Member of the Court Shebek, and instead of crying or exchanging caresses, Ivan Ilyich puts on a serious, stern, thoughtful aspect and, by force of habit, expresses and stubbornly defends his opinion on a decision handed down by the Court of Cassation. The presence of this lie, all around him and within him, did more than anything to poison the final days of Ivan Ilyich's life.

## VIII

It was morning. It must have been morning because Gerasim had left and Pyotr the footman had come in and put out the candles, drawn back one of the curtains and begun to tidy up. Whether it was morning or evening, Friday or Sunday, no longer mattered. It was all the same now, always the same: the gnawing, tormenting pain that would not for a moment subside; the awareness of life slipping hopelessly away but not yet gone; the approach of terrible, loathsome death—the only reality; and always the same lie. Days, weeks, hours, what did they matter now?

"Would master like some tea?"

*He needs routine—needs the gentlefolk to drink tea in the morning*, thought Ivan Ilyich, but said only:

"No."

"Wouldn't master like to move to the sofa?"

*He needs to tidy up the room, and I'm in the way—to him I'm filth, disorder*, he thought, but said only:

"No, let me be."

The footman kept bustling about. Ivan Ilyich reached out his hand. Pyotr approached, ready to help.

"What would the master like?"

"My watch."

Pyotr picked up the watch, which was close at hand, and gave it to Ivan Ilyich.

"Half past eight. Are they up?"

"No, no they aren't, sir. Vasily Ivanovich"—Ivan

Ilyich's son—"has gone off to school, and Praskovya Fyodorovna ordered me to wake her if master asked for her. Would master like me to wake her?"

"No, don't." *Shouldn't I try some tea?* he thought. "Yes, tea… Bring me some tea."

Pyotr went to the door. Ivan Ilyich had come to dread being alone. *How can I keep him here? Yes, the medicine.* "Pyotr, give me my medicine." *Why not? It might still help.* He took the spoonful and drank it. *No, it won't help. It's all nonsense, deception,* he decided as soon as he experienced that familiar, sickly-sweet, hopeless taste. *No, I can't force myself to believe it any longer. But the pain, the pain… For a single minute without pain…* And he began to moan. Pyotr returned. "No, go—go bring me some tea."

Pyotr went out. Now by himself, Ivan Ilyich moaned not so much from pain—although the pain was terrible—as from anguish. *All the same, always the same, the endless nights and days. Oh, I wish it would hurry.* What *would hurry? Death… Darkness… No, no—anything is better than death.*

When Pyotr came in with the tea on a tray, Ivan Ilyich gazed at him blankly for a long time, not understanding who or what he was. This gaze confused and embarrassed Pyotr, and when Pyotr grew embarrassed, Ivan Ilyich came to his senses.

"Yes, tea," he said. "Very good… Set it down. Just help me wash and put on a clean shirt."

Ivan Ilyich began to wash. With pauses for rest, he washed his hands and his face, brushed his teeth, then began to comb his hair and looked in the mirror. He was frightened by what he saw; what frightened him most was the way his hair lay flat on his pale forehead.

As his shirt was being changed he knew that a glance at his body would prove still more frightening, so he avoided looking at himself. But then it was over. He put on his robe, covered himself with a rug and sat down in the armchair to drink his tea. For a moment he felt refreshed, but as soon as he took a sip, there they were—that same taste, that same pain. He forced himself to finish, then lay down again, stretching out his legs. He lay down and dismissed Pyotr.

The same thing, always: a glimmering drop of hope, drowned out by a raging sea of despair and always, constantly, the pain—the constant pain, the constant anguish, always the same. It was terribly depressing to be alone; he always wanted to call someone, but he knew that the presence of others was still more depressing. *Another dose of morphine— better oblivion… The doctor has to come up with something else. This is impossible, impossible.*

An hour passes, two hours—but then the doorbell rings. The doctor? Yes. And here he is, fresh, vigorous, plump, cheerful, with an expression that seems to say, *Well, you've given yourself quite a fright, but we'll sort it all out.* The doctor knows that this expression is out of place here, but having put it on for good and all, he can no longer remove it, like a man who has put on a tailcoat in the morning and gone out to pay calls.

The doctor rubs his hands vigorously, reassuringly.

"It's a cold one out there. I tell you, that frost means business. Let me warm up a bit," he says, as if to suggest that it is only a matter of waiting until he is warm, at which point he will set everything right.

"Well, how...?"

Ivan Ilyich senses that the doctor wants to say, *How's it going?* but that he too feels this would be inappropriate, so he says instead: "How was your night?"

Ivan Ilyich gives the doctor a look that asks: *Will you really never feel ashamed for lying to my face?* But the doctor does not want to acknowledge this question.

And so Ivan Ilyich says:

"Awful, as always. The pain won't stop, won't relent. Please think of something, anything."

"Yes, that's what you sick people always say. Well, now I seem to be warm enough. Even the scrupulous Praskovya Fyodorovna would voice no objection to my temperature. Good morning, sir," and the doctor presses Ivan Ilyich's hand.

Then, abandoning his former playfulness, the doctor begins to examine his patient with a serious air, feeling his pulse and his temperature, tapping and auscultating.

Ivan Ilyich knows beyond a doubt that all this is nonsense and hollow deception. But when the doctor kneels beside him, placing his ear first higher, then lower, and, with a most significant countenance, makes various gymnastic movements over his body, Ivan Ilyich gives in to it, just as he had sometimes given in to the speeches of lawyers when he knew full well that they were lying and why they were lying.

The doctor, kneeling on the sofa, is still tapping away when Praskovya Fyodorovna's silk dress rustles at the door and she is heard reproaching Pyotr for not informing her of the doctor's arrival.

She enters, kisses her husband, and immediately begins to assert that she has been up for ages and only failed to be there when the doctor arrived because of a misunderstanding.

Ivan Ilyich looks at her, examines her from top to toe, resenting and blaming her for the whiteness, plumpness and cleanliness of her hands and neck, the gloss of her hair and the glitter of her eyes, which are brimming with life. He hates her with all his heart. And he suffers from a rising tide of hatred at her touch.

Her attitude towards him and his illness is unchanging. Just as the doctor had worked out an attitude towards his patients that he could no longer shake off, so had she developed an unshakable attitude towards her husband—that he was not doing something he ought to be doing, that it was all his own fault, and that she was lovingly admonishing him for it.

"He simply won't listen to me! Never takes his medicine on time. And worst of all, he lies in a position that is probably quite harmful to him—with his legs up."

She describes how he makes Gerasim hold his legs.

The doctor smiles with affable condescension, as if to say: *What can you do? These sick people come up with all sorts of bosh, but that can be forgiven.*

When the examination was over, the doctor glanced at his watch, and then Praskovya Fyodorovna announced to Ivan Ilyich that he, of course, could do as he pleased, but she had invited a celebrated specialist to come to the house that day, and this specialist and Mikhail Danilovich (the name of the ordinary doctor) would look him over together and discuss his case.

"Please don't resist. I'm doing this for my sake," she said ironically, letting it be felt that she was doing it all for his sake and had only said otherwise so as to deprive him of the right to refuse. He knit his brows and remained silent. The lie surrounding him, he sensed, had got so tangled that it was hard to make out anything at all.

Everything she put him through was done strictly for her own sake, and she told him she did it for her own sake as if the assertion were so incredible that its opposite must be true.

And indeed, at half past eleven, the celebrated specialist arrived. Again there were auscultations and significant conversations in his presence and in the other room concerning the kidney and the blind gut, and enquiries and responses issued with such an air of importance that, once again, in place of the real question of life and death, which was now the only question before him, there emerged the question of the kidney and the blind gut, which were behaving improperly and upon which Mikhail Danilovich and the celebrity were ready to pounce at any moment, so as to force them to mend their ways.

LEO TOLSTOY

The celebrated specialist bade farewell with a serious but not altogether hopeless expression on his face. And to the timid question that Ivan Ilyich, his eyes glistening with fear and hope, raised as to whether there was a possibility of recovery, he replied that, though he could not vouch for it, such a possibility existed. The hopeful gaze with which Ivan Ilyich watched the doctor leave was so pitiful that, upon seeing it, Praskovya Fyodorovna even broke into tears as she went out to hand the celebrated specialist his fee.

The heartening effect of the specialist's reassurance did not last long. Again the same room, the same pictures, curtains, wallpaper, vials and the same aching, suffering body. Ivan Ilyich began to moan; he was given an injection and drifted into oblivion.

When he came to, it was twilight. He was served dinner and forced down some broth—and then again it was the same as always and another night approached.

After dinner, at seven o'clock, Praskovya Fyodorovna came into his room in evening dress, with her large breasts corseted and with traces of powder on her face. She had reminded him in the morning of their trip to the theatre. Sarah Bernhardt was in town and they had a box that he had insisted they take. Now he had forgotten about it and her attire offended him. But he concealed his resentment when he remembered that he himself had insisted on their engaging a box and going, because it would be an educative aesthetic pleasure for the children.

Praskovya Fyodorovna came in looking self-satisfied yet somehow guilty. She sat down and asked about his health—but he saw that she asked this simply for the sake of asking, not in order to find out, for she knew there was nothing to find out—and then she proceeded to tell him what she needed to say: that she would not have gone for anything in the world, but they had already engaged the box, and Helen and their daughter and Petrishchev (the examining magistrate, their daughter's fiancé) were going, and she could not, of course, let them go alone... Although she would have much preferred to sit here with him. And he should be careful to follow the doctor's instructions while she was away.

"Oh, and Fyodor Petrovich"—the fiancé—"would like to come in. May he? And Liza too."

"Very well."

The daughter came in dressed in the finest fashion, baring her youthful flesh—the same flesh that made him suffer so. And here she was, exhibiting it. She was strong, healthy, obviously in love and indignant at the illness, suffering and death that stood in the way of her happiness.

Fyodor Petrovich came in too, wearing a tailcoat, with his hair curled *à la Capoul*,[9] a white collar tight about his long, sinewy neck, an enormous white shirtfront, narrow black trousers clinging to his strong thighs, and one hand in a white glove, holding his opera hat.

The schoolboy crept in behind him, poor little fellow, wearing a new uniform and gloves. He had awful blue shadows under his eyes; Ivan Ilyich knew what that meant.

His son had always seemed pitiful to him. Now the boy's frightened, commiserating gaze terrified him. It seemed to Ivan Ilyich that, besides Gerasim, Vasya alone understood and pitied him.

They all sat down and asked about his health again. This led to silence. Liza asked her mother about the opera glasses. This led to a quarrel between mother and daughter as to where the glasses were and who had put them there. It was all rather unpleasant.

Fyodor Petrovich asked Ivan Ilyich whether he had ever seen Sarah Bernhardt. At first Ivan Ilyich did not quite understand the question, but then he replied: "No. Have you?"

"I have. In *Adrienne Lecouvreur*."

Praskovya Fyodorovna opined that Bernhardt was especially good in such and such a role. The daughter disagreed. This gave rise to a conversation about the elegance and realism of her acting—a conversation that is always exactly the same.

In the midst of this conversation Fyodor Petrovich glanced at Ivan Ilyich and fell silent. Then the others glanced at Ivan Ilyich and also fell silent. Ivan Ilyich was staring straight ahead, with glistening eyes, clearly indignant with them. This had to be set right, but there was no way to set it right. Somehow, the silence had to be broken, but no one dared break it— and they were all growing afraid that the decent, decorous lie might somehow, suddenly, be punctured, that they would all be forced to confront reality. Liza was first to act. She broke the silence. Although she wished to conceal what everyone was feeling, she made it known.

"Well, if we *are* going to go, then we had better go," she said, glancing at her watch, a present from her father. She then gave the young man a barely noticeable smile, which seemed to hint at something known only to them, and rose with a rustle of her dress.

Everyone rose, wished Ivan Ilyich good night, and went out.

When they left the room Ivan Ilyich seemed to feel relief: the lie was gone—they had taken it with them.

But the pain remained—that same pain, that same fear, which made it so that nothing was harder and nothing was easier. Everything was worse.

Again minute followed minute, hour followed hour, and all was the same, there was no end to it, and yet the end was inevitable and grew more and more horrifying.

"Yes, send in Gerasim," he said in response to a question of Pyotr's.

## IX

His wife returned late in the evening. She entered on tiptoe but he heard her coming; he opened his eyes then quickly shut them again. She wanted to send Gerasim away and sit with him herself. He opened his eyes and said: "No. Go."

"Is it very bad?"

"Doesn't matter."

"Take some opium."

He agreed and drank it. She left.

Until about three o'clock he lay in agonizing oblivion. It seemed to him that he was undergoing the painful process of being stuffed into a black bag, narrow and deep—that he was being pushed ever further into the bag, but could not be pushed through completely. And this terrible process was causing him great suffering. He was afraid but wished to fall in; he struggled but tried to help. And suddenly he broke through, fell and came to his senses. There sat Gerasim, same as before, drowsing quietly, patiently at the foot of the bed. And he himself was lying on his back, with his emaciated, stockinged legs on Gerasim's shoulders. There was the same shaded candle, and the same incessant pain.

"Go, Gerasim," he whispered.

"It's no trouble, sir—I'll stay."

"No, go."

He lowered his legs, turned sideways onto his arm, and suddenly felt sorry for himself. He waited until Gerasim had gone into the next room, then he let himself go and began to weep like a child. He wept over his helplessness and his terrible loneliness, over people's cruelty, over God's cruelty, over the absence of God.

*Why have You done all this? Why have You brought me here? What... what have I done to deserve this unbearable torment at Your hands?*

He expected no answer, yet he wept that there was not and could not be an answer. The pain became more violent again, but he did not move, did not call for help. He went on talking to himself: *Go on, then—beat me! But what for? What have I done to You? Why?*

Then he grew quiet and not only stopped weeping but stopped breathing and was all attention—as if he were listening not to an audible voice but to the voice of his soul, to the stream of thoughts rising up within him.

*What do you need?* was the first clear, verbally expressible notion he heard. *What do you need? What do you need?* he repeated to himself. *What do I need? Not to suffer. To live*, he replied.

And again he committed himself to a state of such concerted attention that even pain could not distract him.

*To live? To live how?* asked the voice of his soul.

*Yes, to live. To live as I used to live—a good, pleasant life.*

*What was so good and pleasant about your life?* asked the voice. And in his imagination he began to sort through the finest moments of his pleasant life. But, strangely enough, the finest moments of his pleasant life now seemed to be something else entirely, nothing like what they had seemed then—all of them, aside from his earliest childhood memories. There, in childhood, there really had been something pleasant, something with which one might live if it were to return. But the person who had experienced that pleasure no longer existed; it was like remembering someone else.

As soon as he reached the start of what had resulted in him at present, in Ivan Ilyich, those things that had once seemed joys melted before his eyes and turned into something insignificant, often horrid.

And the further he departed from childhood, the closer he came to the present, the more insignificant and dubious were the joys. It began with law school. There he had still found some truly good things: fun, friendship, hope. But in the upper classes such things were already becoming rare. Then, during the first years of his service with the local governor, a few good moments appeared again: these were memories of love for a woman. Then all grew confused and there was even less that was good. Further on there was still less—and the further he went, the less there was.

The marriage... So accidental... The disillusionment, the smell of his wife's breath, the sensuality, the pretence... And the soul-deadening work, the worries about money—a year of that, then two, ten, twenty—all the same. Only more deadening with each step... *It's as if I had been trudging steadily downhill, all the while imagining that I was going uphill.*

*That's precisely how it was. I was going up in public opinion, yet life was slipping away from under me at exactly the same pace… And now it's all done—go ahead and die.*

*But what is this? Why? It can't be… Is life really so senseless, so horrid? And if it is so horrid and senseless, then why die, why die in agony? Something's not right.*

And suddenly it would occur to him: *Maybe I did not live as I ought to have lived?* But then he would say to himself: *How could that be, if I did everything correctly?* And with that he would dismiss the one and only solution to the whole riddle of life and death as something entirely inconceivable.

*So what do you want now? To live? How? To live as you live in court when the bailiff proclaims, "The court is now in session"? The court is in session, the court,* he repeated to himself. "I'm on trial. But I'm not guilty!" he shouted angrily. "What for?" He stopped crying, turned his face to the wall and brooded over that single question: *Why this horror—what is it for?*

But try as he might, he could find no answer. And whenever the thought occurred to him, as it often did, that the horror had stemmed from his not having lived as he ought to have lived, he would immediately recall the impeccable correctness of his life and banish the strange notion from his mind.

X

Two more weeks passed. Ivan Ilyich no longer left the sofa. He did not wish to lie in bed and so he lay on the sofa. He spent nearly the whole time with his face to the wall, tormented in loneliness by the same insoluble suffering, and brooding in loneliness over the same insoluble question: *What is this? Can it truly be death?* And the inner voice would reply: *Yes, it truly is.* He would ask: *Why must I suffer like this?* And the voice would reply: *No reason. That's just how it is.* Beyond and aside from this, there was nothing.

From the very beginning of Ivan Ilyich's illness, since his first visit to the doctor, his life had been divided between two opposite and alternating moods: now it was despair and the expectation of an incomprehensible, terrible death; now it was hope and the fascinated observation of his bodily functions. Now before him appeared only the kidney or gut, which had temporarily shirked its duties, and now only incomprehensible, terrible death, from which he would not escape.

These two moods had alternated from the very beginning of his illness, but as the illness progressed, his notions about the kidney came to seem ever more dubious and fantastic, while his awareness of impending death became ever more real.

It was enough to reflect on what he had been three months earlier and what he was now, to reflect on how steadily he had gone downhill, and every possibility of hope was shattered.

In the latest stages of the loneliness that enveloped him as he lay with his face to the back of the sofa, that loneliness in the midst of a crowded town, his many acquaintances, his family—a loneliness more complete than could be found at the bottom of the sea or deep inside the earth—in the latest stages of this dreadful loneliness Ivan Ilyich lived only in his memories of the past. Images rose before him, one after the other. They always began with what was nearest and led back to what was most remote, to childhood, where they would linger. If Ivan Ilyich should recall the stewed prunes he had been offered that day, he would then recall the raw, shrivelled French plums of his childhood, their special taste and the way his mouth would fill with saliva as he sucked their stones—and the memory of that taste would give rise to a whole series of memories from that time: his nanny, his brother, his toys. *No, don't think about that... it's too painful*, Ivan Ilyich would say to himself and return to the present—to the button on the back of the sofa and the wrinkled morocco. *Morocco is expensive but it doesn't last. We had a quarrel about it. But it was a different kind of morocco and a different quarrel when Father punished us for tearing his briefcase and mama brought us little pies.* And again Ivan Ilyich's thoughts lingered on his childhood, causing him pain, and he tried to banish them, to think of something else.

And again, right alongside that string of recollections, another string worked its way through his soul—memories of how his illness had progressed and grown worse. There, too, the further back he went, the more life there was. There had been more of what was good in life, and more of life itself. The two merged together. *Just as my suffering keeps growing worse and worse, so my whole life kept growing worse and worse,* he thought. There had been one bright spot back there, at the beginning of life, and then it all grew more and more black, more and more quickly. *In inverse proportion to the square of the distance from death,* thought Ivan Ilyich. And that image of a stone falling with ever-increasing speed sank into his soul. Life was a series of increasing torments, hurtling ever more quickly towards its end in the most dreadful of torments. *I'm falling...* He shuddered, stirred and wanted to resist, but he knew that resistance was now impossible; and again, with eyes weary of looking but unable not to look at what lay before them, he stared at the back of the sofa and waited—waited for that dreadful fall, collision and destruction. *There's no resisting it*, he told himself. *But if I could only understand what it's all for… That, too, is impossible. One could explain it by saying that I had not lived as I ought to have lived. But it's impossible to admit that now*, he said to himself, recalling the whole legality, correctness and decency of his life. *It's impossible to admit that*, he said to himself, his lips grinning as if someone could see his smile and be deceived by it. *There is no explanation. Suffering, death… What for?*

## XI

Two weeks passed in this way. During that time there occurred an event that Ivan Ilyich and his wife had desired: Petrishchev made a formal proposal. This happened in the evening. The next day Praskovya Fyodorovna entered her husband's room, pondering how best to announce Fyodor Petrovich's proposal, but that very night Ivan Ilyich's condition had taken another turn for the worse. As usual, Praskovya Fyodorovna found him on the sofa, but in a new position. He lay flat on his back, groaning and staring straight in front of him with fixed eyes.

She began to talk about medicines. He turned his eyes towards her. She did not finish what she had started to say; his eyes were filled with such anger—anger aimed directly at her.

"For Christ's sake, let me die in peace," he said.

She wanted to leave but just then their daughter came in and went up to say good morning. He gave the daughter the same look he had given his wife, and in response to her enquiry about his health drily declared that they would all soon be free of him. They both fell silent, sat a while and left the room.

"How is any of this our fault?" Liza asked her mother. "It's as if we were somehow to blame! I feel sorry for Papa, but why should we be made to suffer?"

The doctor arrived at his usual time. Ivan Ilyich replied to all questions with "yes" or "no", never taking his angry eyes off him, and at the end he said: "You know you can do nothing to help me, so go away."

"We can ease your suffering," said the doctor.

"You can't even do that. Just go away."

The doctor came into the drawing room and told Praskovya Fyodorovna that things looked very bad indeed and that the only possible way to ease her husband's suffering, which must be terrible, was opium.

The doctor meant that Ivan Ilyich's physical suffering was terrible, and this was true; but more terrible than his physical suffering was his moral suffering, the source of his greatest torment.

His moral suffering stemmed from the question that occurred to him that night as he looked at Gerasim's sleepy, good-natured face with its high cheekbones: *Could my whole life—my whole conscious life—have been wrong?*

It occurred to him that what he had formerly imagined to be a perfect impossibility, the notion that he had lived his life not as he ought to have done, could in fact be true. It occurred to him that his faint, feeble impulses to struggle against what the people of highest standing considered to be good—those feeble impulses he had immediately rejected—might have been the real thing, while everything else was false. His professional duties, his mode of life, his family, his social and professional interests—all, all might have been false. He tried to defend it all to himself—but then he suddenly felt the absolute weakness of what he was defending. There was no use defending it.

*But if that's the case*, he said to himself, *and I'm leaving life in the knowledge that I have ruined everything given me, and that it cannot be rectified, what then?* He lay flat on his back and began to sort through his life in an entirely new way. In the morning, when he saw first the footman, then his wife, then his daughter, then the doctor, their every word, every movement confirmed the terrible truth that had been revealed to him during the night. In them he saw himself and everything he had lived for, and he saw clearly that it was all false—it was all a dreadful, enormous lie that concealed both life and death. This knowledge increased his physical suffering tenfold. He groaned and thrashed about and tugged at his clothes, which he felt were choking and stifling him. And for this he hated them all.

He was given a large dose of opium and lost consciousness, but at lunchtime it began again. He sent everyone away and kept tossing from side to side.

His wife came in and said: "Jean, darling, do this for me"—*for me?*—"It won't do any harm, but it often helps. Really, it's nothing. Even perfectly healthy people…"

He opened his eyes wide.

"What? Take communion? What for? No, I don't need… Well, perhaps…"

She began to cry.

"Yes, my dear? I'll send for our priest. He's such a lovely man."

"Yes, yes, very good," he said.

When the priest came and heard his confession, Ivan Ilyich mellowed and believed he felt relief from his doubts and, consequently, from his suffering; for a moment there was hope. He began to think about his blind gut again, about the possibility of setting it right. He received communion with tears in his eyes.

When they laid him down afterwards he felt a moment's relief and, once again, hope that he might live. He began to think of the operation that had been suggested to him. *I want to live, to live*, he was telling himself. His wife came in to congratulate him and, after saying the usual words, added: "You're feeling better, aren't you?"

Without looking at her he replied, "Yes."

Her attire, her posture, the expression on her face, the sound of her voice—they all told him the same thing: *False. Everything you have lived for and continue to live for is a lie—a deception that conceals life and death from you.* And as soon as he thought this, hatred welled up within him—and with the hatred came unbearable physical suffering, and with the suffering came the awareness of inevitable, fast-approaching death.

Something new took hold of him: wrenching, shooting pains that squeezed the breath out of his body.

The expression on his face as he said "Yes" was horrifying. Having said it and looked straight into her eyes, he rolled over with extraordinary speed for a man in his condition and began to shout: "Go away! Go away! Leave me alone!"

XII

From that moment began the howling that did not cease for three days, a howling so terrible that it struck one with horror through two closed doors. At the moment he answered his wife he realized that he was doomed, that there was no going back, that it was over, all over, while his doubts remained unresolved, remained doubts.

"O! O! O!" he howled with various intonations. He had begun by howling "No!"—and continued to howl its last letter, "O".

Throughout those three days time did not exist for him. He was thrashing about inside the black bag into which he was being thrust by an invisible, irresistible force. He struggled as one condemned to death struggles in the hands of the executioner although he knows he will not save himself; with every passing moment he felt that despite all his efforts he was coming closer and closer to what terrified him. He felt that his torment was caused by his being thrust into that black hole and, even more so, by his inability to make it through. He was prevented from making it through by his conviction that his life had been a good one. This justification of his life dug its claws into him, would not let him go forward, and tormented him more than anything else.

All of a sudden some force shoved him in the chest and in the side and made it still more difficult to breathe; he fell into the hole and there, at its bottom, saw a glimmer of light. What he experienced now was like what he had sometimes experienced in railway carriages, when one thinks one is going forward but is actually going backwards, and then suddenly comes to realize the real direction.

*Yes, it was all wrong,* he told himself, *but that's fine. I can still make it "right". I can... But what is "right"?* he asked himself, then suddenly fell silent.

This was at the end of the third day, an hour before his death. Just at that time the schoolboy had quietly crept into his father's room and gone up to his bed. The dying man was howling desperately, flailing his arms. One of his hands landed on the schoolboy's head. The schoolboy seized it, pressed it to his lips and began to cry.

Just at that time Ivan Ilyich fell through, saw the light, and it was revealed to him that his life had not been what it ought to have been but that there was still time to set things right. He asked himself, *What is "right"?* and grew still, listening. And then he felt someone kissing his hand. He opened his eyes and glanced at his son. He felt sorry for him. His wife came closer. He glanced at her. She was watching him with a desperate expression on her face, open-mouthed, with unwiped tears on her nose and cheek. He felt sorry for her too.

*Yes, I'm making them suffer,* he thought. *They feel sorry for me but it will be better for them when I die.* He wanted to say as much but he was simply too weak to get out the words. *In any case, why say it? The thing is to do it,* he thought. He turned his eyes to his son and said to his wife:

"Take him away… sorry for him… for you too…" He wanted to add "Forgive", but said "Forgo" and, too weak to correct himself, waved his hand, knowing that he would be understood by the one who needed to understand.

And suddenly it dawned on him that what had been causing him such torment and would not leave his body was leaving him all at once, from two sides, from ten sides, from all sides. He felt sorry for them and needed to relieve their pain. He needed to free them and to free himself of this suffering. *How good and how simple*, he thought. *And the pain?* he asked himself. *What do I do about it? Let's see... Where are you, pain?*

He turned his attention to it.

*Ah, there it is. All right, so be it.*

*And death? Where is death?*

He was searching for his former habitual fear of death and could not find it. Where was it? What death? There was no fear, because there was no death.

Instead of death there was light.

"So that's it," he suddenly said aloud. "What joy!"

For him all this transpired in an instant, and the meaning of this instant never changed. For those present his agony continued for another two hours. There was a gurgling in his chest and his emaciated body trembled. Then the gurgling and wheezing grew less and less frequent.

"It's over," said someone over him.

He heard these words and repeated them in his soul. *Death is over*, he told himself. *No more death.*

He drew in air, stopped midway through the breath, stretched out, and died.

# PACE-SETTER

## *The Story of a Horse*

IN MEMORY OF M.A. STAKHOVICH[1]

### I

THE SKY ROSE higher and higher, the dawn spread wider and wider, and the dull silvery drops of dew turned ever more white. Life was fading from the crescent moon, while the forest was slowly filling with noise. People were starting their day, and in the master's stable yard the sounds of rustling straw, of snorting and even of shrill angry neighing among squabbling horses grew ever more frequent.

"Come on! Get back! Hungry, eh?" said the old herdsman, opening the creaking gate. "I said get back!" he shouted, waving his arm at a little mare that was making for the gate.

Nester the herdsman wore a Cossack coat. He had a whip over his shoulder and some bread wrapped in cloth stuck in his ornamented belt. He was carrying a saddle and bridle.

The horses were not at all frightened or offended by his mocking tone. In fact, they pretended not to care and slowly walked away from the gate. Only one old mare—dark bay, with a thick mane—pinned back her ear and swiftly turned round, showing him her rear. At that point a young filly that was standing behind her and was not at all involved in the matter suddenly whinnied and kicked out at the nearest horse.

"Come on!" the herdsman cried out even louder and more sternly, then made his way towards the corner of the yard.

Of all the horses in the enclosure (there were about a hundred of them), a piebald gelding who stood alone in the corner showed the least impatience. He stood under a canopy, squinting and licking an oak post. It is impossible to say what flavour he found in that post, but the expression on his face as he licked it was thoughtful and serious.

"Enough!" the herdsman shouted in the same tone, approaching the gelding and placing the saddle and a glossy saddlecloth on the manure heap beside him.

The gelding stopped licking and stared at Nester for a long time, not moving a muscle. He neither laughed, nor got angry, nor frowned, but only heaved a huge sigh with his whole belly, then turned away. The herdsman wrapped his arms around the gelding's neck and put on the bridle.

"Whatcha sighing for?" he asked.

The gelding switched his tail as if to say: "Nothing, Nester. Nothing." When Nester put on the saddle-cloth and saddle, the gelding pinned back his ears, evidently to express his displeasure. This did no good: he was only called a "lousy bastard" and the saddle girths were drawn tighter. The gelding puffed himself up—but a finger was thrust in his mouth and he was kneed in the belly, so that he had to let out his breath. Nevertheless, when Nester was cinching the strap with his teeth, the gelding again pinned back his ears and even looked round. Although he knew it would do no good, he still thought it necessary to show his displeasure and to make it clear that he would always show it. When he was finally saddled he put his swollen right leg forward and began champing at his bit; this too he did for some special reason of his own, since he surely knew by then that bits have no flavour.

Nester put his foot in the short stirrup and mounted the gelding, unwound his whip, pulled the side of his coat from under his knee, positioned himself in that special coachman-huntsman-herdsman manner, and tugged the reins. The gelding raised his head, indicating his willingness to go where he was ordered to go, but did not move. He knew that before riding, the man atop of him still had more shouting to do; there would be orders for the horses and the other herdsman, Vaska. And Nester did indeed commence shouting: "Vaska! Hey, Vaska! Did ya let out the brood mares? Whatcha doin'—sleepin', you dog? Get a move on and open the gate! Let them brood mares out first," and so on.

The gate creaked. Vaska, sleepy and irritated, stood by the gatepost. He held his horse by the bridle and let the other animals past, one by one. Stepping carefully on the straw and sniffing at it, they filed out: fillies, yearlings, suckling foals and pregnant mares cautiously carrying their heavy wombs through the gate. The fillies sometimes huddled in twos or threes, laying their heads across each other's backs and trying to hurry through; for this they were chided nastily by the herdsmen. The suckling foals sometimes dashed under the legs of the wrong mares, neighing loudly in response to their mothers' short whinnies.

As soon as she was past the gate, the frisky filly bent her head down and to the side, kicked up her hind legs and squealed; still, she did not dare to race out in front of old Zhuldyba, grey and dappled, who with slow, heavy tread, shifting her belly from side to side, walked as always ahead of all the other horses.

In just a few minutes the enclosure, which had been so full of life, stood sadly empty; posts stuck up gloomily under deserted canopies; there was nothing around but trampled straw, matted with manure. Although the piebald gelding must have been used to this desolate scene, it still appeared to depress him. Slowly, as if bowing, he lowered and lifted his head, sighed as deeply as the tightened strap would allow him and hobbled along after the herd on his stiff, crooked legs, bearing old Nester on his bony back.

*I know that as soon as we're out on the road he'll strike fire and light that wooden pipe of his, with its brass mounting and little chain,* thought the gelding. *And I'm glad. It makes a pleasant smell, early in the morning, mixed with the dew. Brings to mind many pleasant things. The only trouble is that when the old man sticks that pipe in his mouth he gets ideas, thinks he's somebody, and then he sits sideways, always sideways—but my side hurts. Oh, well, let him sit how he wants—nothing new in my suffering for the enjoyment of others. I've even begun to find a certain equine pleasure in it.*

*After all, the poor fellow can only swagger when there's no
one around, so let him sit sideways,* reasoned the gelding
and, stepping carefully on his battered legs, walked
along the middle of the road.

## II

Having driven the horses to the riverside where they
were to graze, Nester climbed down from the gelding
and unsaddled him. The herd had already begun to
disperse through the untrampled meadow, which
was covered with dew and with a mist that rose both
from the grass and from the river winding round it.

After removing the gelding's bridle, Nester gave
him a little scratch under the neck, in response to
which, as a sign of gratitude and pleasure, the gelding closed his eyes. "The old dog likes it," Nester
muttered. In truth, the gelding found no pleasure
whatsoever in this scratching and only pretended that
he enjoyed it out of courtesy; yet he shook his head in
agreement. But then, completely unexpectedly and
for no reason at all, Nester—who assumed, perhaps,
that too much familiarity might give the gelding a
false sense of importance—pushed away the horse's
head and, swinging the bridle, struck the gelding's

bad leg painfully with its buckle. And without saying another word, he went up the hillock towards the stump beside which he usually sat.

The sudden blow grieved the piebald gelding but he did not show it; slowly switching his sparse tail, sniffing at this and that and nibbling at the grass only to distract himself, he made his way to the river. He paid no attention to the young fillies, colts and foals basking joyously in the morning sun; knowing that it was healthiest, especially at his age, to have a good drink before eating, he chose the widest and shallowest spot on the bank, wet his hooves and fetlocks, dipped his muzzle into the water and sucked it up through his torn lips, expanding his sides and happily switching his paltry tail with its bare stump.

Soon the feisty chestnut filly who always teased and bullied the old fellow came close to him, making as if she was attending to some business of her own, when in reality her only intent had been to muddy the water in front of his nose. But the gelding had already drunk his fill and, as if ignorant of the filly's motivation, calmly drew one foot after the other from the mud, shook his head, stepped away from the youngsters and began to eat. Planting his legs wide apart in various ways, so as not to trample any more grass than necessary, he ate without lifting his head for three hours straight. Having stuffed himself until his belly hung like a sack from his firm, skinny ribs, he positioned his sore legs so that each of them would feel as little pain as possible—especially the right foreleg, which was the weakest—and fell asleep.

Old age can be majestic or it can be ugly; and it can be miserable. But it can also be ugly and majestic at the same time. Such was the piebald gelding's old age.

The gelding was tall, nearly sixteen hands high. His coat was white with black spots—or had been, since the spots had long ago faded to a dirty brown. There were three of them. The first spot was on the head, extending from a crooked bald spot on the side of the nose to halfway down the neck. His long mane, tangled with burrs, was partly white, partly brownish. Another spot stretched along his off side to the middle of his belly. The third was on the croup, encompassing the upper part of the tail and half his thighs. The rest of the tail was whitish, also dotted with spots. His large bony head, with its deep hollows above the eyes and a saggy, torn black lip, hung low and heavy on a lean and bent neck that looked like a piece of wood. The saggy lip revealed a blackish tongue pressed to the side and the yellow remnants of the lower teeth. The ears, one of which had been slit, drooped limply; only occasionally would they move, half-heartedly, to flick away a fly. A single long tuft of the forelock was tucked behind an ear; the bare forehead was dented and rough; and loose bags of skin hung from the broad jawbones. The veins on the neck and head stood out in knots that shuddered and trembled at the slightest touch of a fly. The expression of his face was sternly patient, deeply thoughtful and pained. His forelegs were bent like bows at the knees; there was swelling above both hooves, and on one leg, where the spot reached halfway down, a bump near the knee the size of a fist. The hind legs were less weathered, but his thighs had apparently been rubbed bald so long ago that hair would never cover them again. And all four legs seemed disproportionately long, on account of his skinniness. His ribs, though firm, stood out so starkly and were so tightly bound that the hide seemed to stick fast to the hollows between them. His back and withers bore the traces of old whippings and there was a fresh sore on his rear, still swollen and festering. The long black dock of his tail, with the vertebrae showing distinctly, stuck out behind him, almost bare. On the brown croup, near the tail, was a scar in the shape of a human palm, like a bite, overgrown with white hair; there was another scar on his shoulder. His hocks and tail were soiled as a result of chronic diarrhoea. The hair all over his body, though short, stood up straight. And yet, despite his repulsive old age, when looking at this horse one could not help but think—and an expert would immediately say—that he had, in his day, been a remarkably fine animal.

An expert would even say that there was only one breed in all of Russia that could provide such broad bones, such enormous thighs, such hooves, such slender legs, such a shapely neck and, most of all, such a skull, such eyes—big, black and clear—with such thoroughbred clusters of veins on head and neck, such excellent skin and hair. Indeed, there was something majestic in the figure of this horse, something majestic in the terrible combination he presented of repellent signs of decrepitude—intensified by the motley colour of his coat—and of the calm, self-confident manner that accompanies beauty and strength.

Like a living ruin, he stood alone in the middle of the dewy meadow, while a short distance away sounded the trampling and snorting, the youthful whinnies and neighs of the scattered herd.

III

The sun had climbed above the forest and its light now sparkled brightly on the grass and the winding river. The dew was drying and gathering in droplets; here and there, by the swamp and above the forest, the last of the morning mist rose and faded like smoke. Small clouds grew curly high in the sky, but there was still no wind. Beyond the river, the green rye sprung from the ground in tight little tubes, like stubble, and everything smelt of fresh growth and blossom. From deep in the woods came the hoarse cry of a cuckoo, and Nester, sprawled out upon his back, counted its calls to determine how many years he had left. Larks flew over the rye and the meadow. A belated hare, finding himself amid the herd, leapt into the open meadow, sat himself beside a bush and pricked up his ears. Vaska dozed off with his head in the grass, while the fillies made a still wider circle about him and spread out over the pasture below. The old mares, snorting, laid slick tracks through the dew, each selecting a spot where no one would disturb her; they no longer ate, however, but merely nibbled at the tasty grasses. Imperceptibly, the whole herd was moving in the same direction. Once again, it was old Zhuldyba who, walking sedately ahead of the others, demonstrated the possibility of going forward. Young black Mushka, who had foaled for the first time, kept neighing and, with tail upraised, snorting at her purplish foal who hobbled beside her on quivering legs. The dark bay maiden mare Birdy, smooth and shiny as satin, stood with her head down, her black silky forelock covering her eyes, and toyed with the grass—nipping a tuft, tossing it aside and stamping her leg with its shaggy, dew-drenched fetlock. One of the older foals, evidently playing some game of his own invention, raised his curly little tail like a peacock's plume and, for the twenty-sixth time, galloped round his mother, who, used to her son's personality, went on calmly grazing and only occasionally looked askance at him with her large black eye. One of the very youngest foals, black and big-headed, with a forelock that stuck up in surprise and a little tail that was still bent to the side as it had been in his mother's belly, stood motionless, his ears and dull eyes fixed on the frolicsome, caper-cutting foal, and there was no telling whether he envied or condemned him. Some foals were sucking, prodding their mothers' udders with their noses; others would, for no discernible reason, ignore their mothers' calls and run at an awkward little trot in the very opposite direction, as if searching for something, and then, again for no discernible reason, would stop and neigh in a shrill, desperate voice. A few lay on their sides; some were learning to graze; some were scratching themselves behind their ears with their hind legs. Two mares in foal were walking at a distance from the rest—stepping slowly, one leg at a time, and still grazing. It was clear that the herd respected their condition, and none of the youngsters dared to approach and disturb them. And if some frisky foal so much as thought of coming close, one flick of an ear or tail sufficed to show the rascal how improper that would be.

The yearling colts and fillies pretended they were grown up and sedate. They jumped only rarely and did not join up with the merry bands cavorting around them; they spent their time grazing decorously, arching their close-cropped, swan-like necks and waving about their little whisks as if they were full tails. Just like the grown-ups, some of them lay down on the ground, rolling about or scratching one another. The merriest of the bands was made up of two- and three-year-old maiden mares. Almost all of these merry virgins flocked close together, apart from the rest, and went about stamping and kicking, neighing and whinnying. They would lay their heads across each other's backs, sniff at one another, jump about, and sometimes, throwing their tails straight up with a snort, would proudly and coquettishly parade in front of their companions at a half-trot, half-amble. The most beautiful among them—and the leader of the pack—was the feisty chestnut filly. Whatever pranks she came up with the others played along; wherever she went the others followed. The feisty young thing was in a particularly playful mood that morning. A spirit of joy seized her as it might seize a person. While still at the watering place, after playing a prank on the old gelding, she had taken off running through the water, pretending to be frightened of something, then gave a snort and raced into the meadow as fast as she could, so that Vaska had to gallop after her and all the others who had followed her. Then, having eaten a little, she began to roll about and then to tease the old mares by strutting in front of them. After that, she drove a little foal away from his mother and began to chase him around, as if she wanted to bite him; the mother took fright and stopped grazing, while the little foal kept squealing in a pitiful voice, but the feisty filly did not even touch him—she only meant to scare him and put on a show for her companions, who watched her exploits with approval. Her next goal was to turn the head of a little roan horse with which a peasant was ploughing the rye land far across the river. She halted, proudly lifted her head, cocking it a little on one side, shook herself and began to neigh in a sweet, gentle, drawn-out voice. There was mischief in that neighing, and feeling, and a certain sadness. It expressed both the desire and promise of love, as well as love's sorrow.

A corncrake darted back and forth through the thick reeds, passionately calling for its mate; the cuckoo and the quail both sang of love; and even the flowers exchanged their fragrant dust on the wind.

"I too am young and beautiful and strong," the feisty filly's neighing said. "But I have yet to taste the sweetness of this feeling... Not only have I yet to taste it, but not a single lover—not a single one—has ever laid eyes on me."

And this neighing—freighted with meaning, youthful and sad—resounded over to the lowland and the meadow, finally reaching the little roan horse. He pricked up his ears and halted. The peasant kicked him with one of his bast shoes, but the little horse was enchanted by the silvery sound of the distant neighing and began to neigh in response. The peasant got angry, pulled at the reins and kicked him so hard in the belly that he couldn't finish his neigh and walked on. But the little roan horse had tasted sweetness and sorrow, and for a long time the sounds of passionate neighing cut short by the peasant's angry voice were wafted over to the herd from the distant rye land.

If the sound of her voice alone had made the little roan horse lose his head and forget his duty, what would have happened had he seen the mischievous beauty in all her splendour—calling out to him with her ears cocked, her nostrils flaring and sucking in the air, her entire body, lovely and young, yearning to gallop, trembling?

But the feisty one never gave much thought to the impression she made on others. When the little roan horse's voice died away she uttered a few more mocking neighs, lowered her head and pawed at the ground, then went off to wake and tease the piebald gelding. The gelding was the constant martyr and laughing stock of the happy youngsters. They caused him more grief than people. He did no harm to either. People, of course, needed him, but what drove the young horses to torment him?

IV

He was old and they were young; he was lean and they were fit; he was dull and they were gay. And so he was a total stranger to them, an outsider, a different creature altogether; they could not pity him. Horses can only pity themselves and, occasionally, those in whose hides they can easily imagine themselves. Yet was it the gelding's fault that he was old and lean and ugly? No, it would seem. But horse sense said otherwise: he was indeed to blame, and only those who were young, strong and happy were right—those whose whole lives lay before them, whose every muscle quivered with excess energy, whose tails stood erect. It may be that the gelding himself understood this and, in his quiet moments, agreed that he was guilty of having lived out his life and that he had to pay for it; yet he was still a horse, and often he could not suppress his feelings of resentment, sadness and indignation when he saw these youngsters punishing him so viciously for what would befall them all at life's end. Another cause of the other horses' cruelty was their aristocratic sentiment. Every last one of them could trace their paternal or maternal pedigree back to the famous Creamy, while the piebald gelding was of unknown origin; he was an interloper, bought at a fair three years ago for eighty paper roubles.

The chestnut filly, as if simply taking a stroll, walked right up to the gelding's nose and bumped it. He knew straightaway what was happening and, without opening his eyes, pinned back his ears and bared his teeth. The filly whirled around and made as if she were about to kick him. He opened his eyes and walked away. No longer sleepy, he began to graze. The troublemaker approached the gelding once more, this time accompanied by her girlfriends. A two-year-old, bald-faced little filly—quite stupid, and ever the chestnut's follower and imitator—came up with her and, in the manner of all imitators, began to outdo the instigator. The chestnut filly would usually walk up to the gelding as if going about her business and would pass right by his nose, without so much as glancing at him, so that he did not know whether to be angry or not—and this really was funny. That is exactly what she did now, but her bald-faced follower, who was feeling especially frisky, slammed right into the gelding with her breast. He bared his teeth again, gave a sharp whinny, and, with an agility no one could have expected from him, lunged at her and bit her flank. The young filly kicked the old fellow hard in his skinny, protruding ribs with both her hind legs. He began to wheeze. Although he wanted to lunge at her again, he thought better of it and, with a heavy sigh, walked away. All the youngsters must have taken personal offence at how audaciously the piebald gelding had allowed himself to behave towards the bald-faced filly, and for the rest of the day they would not let him eat or enjoy a moment's peace, so that the herdsman had to restrain the horses several times and could not understand what had got into their heads. This all upset the gelding to such a degree that when Nester was getting ready to drive the herd back, he went up to the old man himself and felt happier and more peaceful after he was saddled and mounted.

God knows what the old gelding was thinking as he bore old Nester away on his back. Did he dwell bitterly on the persistent cruelty of the young, or did he forgive his offenders with the contemptuous, silent pride of the aged? In any case, he kept his thoughts to himself the whole way home. That evening, as Nester drove the herd past the huts on the estate, he noticed a horse and cart tethered to his porch. Some friends had come to see him. He was in such a hurry to get to them that he hustled the gelding into the yard without removing his saddle, shut the gate and shouted to Vaska that he should unsaddle him. Whether because of the offence the "mangy filth", who had been bought at a fair and knew nothing of his parentage, had caused to the bald-faced filly, a great-granddaughter of Creamy, and the offence this had caused to the aristocratic sentiment of the entire herd, or because the gelding, in his high saddle with no rider, presented such a weirdly fantastic spectacle to the other horses, in any event something extraordinary happened that night. All the horses, young and old, chased the gelding round and round with bared teeth; the yard resounded with the crashing of hooves against his skinny ribs and with heavy grunting. He could not take it any more, could no longer evade the blows. He stopped in the middle of the yard, his face at first expressing the repulsive weak rancour of helpless old age, then simply despair; he pinned back his ears and suddenly did something that made all the other horses fall silent. The very oldest mare, Vyazopurikha, approached the gelding, sniffed him and sighed. The gelding sighed too.

V

In the middle of the moonlit stable yard stood the tall, raw-boned figure of the gelding in his high saddle with its jutting pommel. The other horses stood around him, motionless and profoundly silent, as if he had revealed to them something new and extraordinary. They did indeed learn something new and unexpected.

This is what they learnt.

## First Night

—

YES, I'M THE SON of Gracious I and Baba. The name on my pedigree is Mujik I. That's the name on my pedigree, but the crowd gave me a different name, Pace-setter, on account of my long, swinging stride—a stride no horse in all of Russia could ever match. No horse in all the world is of purer blood. I wouldn't have told you any of this. What good would it have done? You wouldn't have recognized me. Even Vyazopurikha, who was with me in Khrenovoye,[2] didn't recognize me until now. And if Vyazopurikha hadn't vouched for me, you still wouldn't have believed me. I would never have told you. I don't need your equine pity. But you asked for it. So yes, I am that Pace-setter: the Pace-setter whom the experts hunt for in vain—the Pace-setter whom the count himself knew and sold off from his stud farm because I outran Swan, his favourite.

When I was born, I had no idea what "piebald" meant. All I knew was I was a horse. The first remark about my coat, I remember, struck me and Mother deeply. I was born at night, it seems, and by morning Mother had licked me clean and I was already on my feet. I remember wanting—wanting something all the time; everything seemed at once very surprising and very simple. Our stalls opened

135

onto a long warm corridor and had lattice doors through which you could see. Mother was offering me her teats, but I was still so innocent that I kept poking my nose under her front legs or under the manger. Suddenly she turned her head to the door and, lifting her leg over my head, stepped aside. The groom on duty was watching us through the lattice.

"Hey, look at that! Baba's gone and foaled," he said. Then he opened the latch, walked across the fresh bedding, and put his arms around me. "Look here, Taras!" he shouted. "Piebald little fella, ain't he? A real magpie."

I tore away from him and stumbled onto my knees.

"Little devil," he said.

Mother grew anxious, but she didn't come to my defence. She only sighed, very heavily, and stepped further away. The other grooms gathered to look at me; one of them ran to tell the stable master. They all laughed at my spots and gave me all sorts of strange names; neither I nor Mother knew the meaning of any of those words. There had never been a single piebald in my line, not a single one among all my relatives. But we didn't see anything bad in it. After all, even then, all the grooms praised my strength, my shape.

"Plenty of fight in him," said the one who had found me. "Can't keep him still."

In a little while the stable master came. He showed surprise at my colour—it even seemed to upset him.

"Who does this little freak take after?" he asked. "The count won't keep him at the stud, that's for sure. Hell, Baba, you've done me a bad turn," he said to Mother. "Even a bald-faced foal would've been better than this spotted beast!"

Mother didn't answer. As always on such occasions, she simply sighed.

"What ugly devil does he take after? A rotten peasant, a proper *mujik*," he continued. "Can't leave him in the stud. He'd bring shame on all of us. But he's a fine little foal, very fine," is what he said—is what everyone said when they looked at me. A few days later the count himself came to see me, and again everyone was horrified, scolding me and Mother for the colour of my coat. "But he's a fine foal, very fine," they all kept saying.

Until spring we all lived in separate stalls in the brood mares' stable, each with his mother. Sometimes, when the sun had already grown warm enough to melt the snow on the roofs, we'd be let out with our mothers into a big yard filled with fresh straw. This is where I first got to know my relations, near and distant. This is where I saw all the famous mares of the day emerging from different doors with their foals. There was old Dutch, and Fly (a daughter of Creamy's), and Ruddy, and the riding horse Well-wisher—all the celebrities. They gathered there with their foals, walked about in the sunshine, rolled around in the fresh straw, sniffed at each other—just like ordinary horses. To this very day I cannot forget the sight of that yard, full of the era's great beauties. It's hard for you to imagine that I too was once young and frisky, but it's true. Your Vyazopurikha was there—just a yearling back then—a lovely, cheerful and frisky filly. But—and I don't say this to offend her—though you now look on her as a horse of the rarest breeding, she was a runt when compared to her peers. She herself will admit it.

My spots, which people found so ugly, seemed to delight the other horses. They would surround me, admire me, flirt and frisk with me. I began to forget what people had said about my spots, began to feel happy. But soon I would have my first experience of grief, and its cause was Mother. When the thaw had set in, and sparrows were chirping away under the canopy, and spring was making itself felt in the air, a change came over her; she began to treat me differently. It seemed she was a different horse altogether. At times she would, for no reason at all, begin to frolic, running around the yard—behaviour terribly out of keeping with her venerable age. Or she might sink into thought and begin to neigh. At other times she would bite and kick at her sister mares, or sniff at me, snorting with displeasure, or walk out into the sun and lay her head across the shoulders of her cousin, Merchant's Wife and, for a long while, scratch the horse's back absentmindedly, pushing me away from her teats. One day the stable master came. He had her haltered and led out of the stall. She neighed and I responded, rushing after her—but she never looked back at me. The groom Taras grabbed hold of me as they were shutting the door behind her. I broke free, laying him out on his back in the straw—but the door had been locked, and all I could hear were Mother's neighs receding into the distance. Yet what I heard in that neighing was no longer a call—it was something else. Then a powerful voice answered hers from afar—the voice, I learnt later, of Kindly I, being led by a groom on each side to meet her. I don't remember Taras leaving my stall; I was too sad to notice. I felt I had lost my mother's love forever. *And all because I am piebald,* I thought, recalling what people had said about my coat—and then I was seized with such anger that I began to beat my head and knees against the walls, and I went on doing it until I was dripping with sweat and completely exhausted.

After some time, Mother came back to me. I heard her trotting up to our stall through the corridor. Her gait sounded strange to me. They opened the door and I did not recognize her—she looked so much younger, so much prettier. She sniffed at me, snorted and began to whinny. I could tell by her expression, her whole manner, that she no longer loved me. She spoke to me of Kindly I—of his beauty, of her love for him. The two of them continued to meet, while our own relationship grew cooler and cooler.

Before long we were let out to pasture and I came to know new joys, which made up for the loss of Mother's love. I had many friends. Together we learnt to graze, to neigh like the grown-ups, to race around our mothers with our tails in the air. It was a happy time. Everyone loved me, admired me, indulged and forgave me, no matter what I did. But it didn't last long. Yes, a terrible thing happened to me…

—

The gelding heaved a deep, deep sigh and walked away from the others.

Morning had broken long ago. The gate creaked open, the herdsman entered and the horses dispersed. Nester straightened the saddle on the gelding's back and drove out the herd.

VI

*Second Night*

As soon as the horses were driven back in they crowded around the piebald again and he continued his story.

—

IN AUGUST I WAS SEPARATED from Mother, but this did not cause me much sorrow. I saw that she was already big with my younger brother, the famed Whiskers, and that I myself was no longer what I had been. I wasn't jealous but I felt myself growing cooler towards her. And besides, I knew that on leaving Mother I would join the general division of foals, where we were kept two or three to a stall and where every day the whole lot of us were let out into the fresh air. I shared a stall with Dear Boy. He was a riding horse and he would later be ridden by the emperor himself—there are paintings of him, statues. But back then he was just an ordinary foal with delicate glossy hair, a swan-like neck and legs as straight and thin as the strings of a violin. Dear Boy was always cheerful, good-natured, amiable—always ready to frisk, swap licks or play little tricks on horses and humans. We couldn't help becoming friends, living together as we did, and our friendship lasted the whole of our youth. He was cheerful and carefree, and already no stranger to love; he flirted with fillies and poked fun at me for my innocence. And to my misfortune, out of sheer vanity, I began to imitate him. And I got carried away—love got the better of me. This early inclination of mine led to the greatest change in my fate. Yes, I got carried away.

Vyazopurikha was one year my senior. She and I were especially good friends. But at the end of the autumn

I noticed that she began to shy away from me… No, I won't give you the whole disastrous story of my first love… She herself remembers my mad passion, which brought about the most important change in my life. The herdsmen rushed to chase her away and to give me a thrashing. In the evening they drove me into a special stall where I neighed all night long, as if I sensed what was to happen the next day.

In the morning the count, the stable master, the grooms and the herdsmen gathered in the corridor outside my stall and raised a terrible racket. The count shouted at the stable master, who tried to defend himself, saying that the grooms had let me out without his permission. The count said that he'd give them all a proper whipping and that you can't keep colts around. The stable master promised that he'd see to everything. Then they quietened down and left. I didn't understand a thing, but I could tell they were plotting something—something about me.

The day after that I stopped neighing forever—I became what I am now. The whole world was transformed in my eyes. Nothing could please me. I withdrew into myself, giving way to dark thoughts. At first, everything repelled me. I wouldn't even drink, wouldn't eat, wouldn't walk, let alone play. From time to time I'd feel the urge to buck, gallop or neigh, but then I'd ask myself that terrible question: Why? What for? And then I'd lose all strength.

One evening I was taken out for a walk just when the herd was being driven back from pasture. They were still far away when I first spotted them—that cloud of dust enveloping the faint but familiar outlines of all our brood mares. I heard the cheerful neighing, the trampling. And I stopped, although the halter and lead rope by which the groom was pulling me cut into the back of my neck. I stopped and gazed at the approaching herd, as one gazes at happiness that is lost forever, never to return. As they came closer I began to make them out, one by one—all those familiar figures, beautiful and stately, healthy and fit. Some of them also looked back at me. I felt no pain from the rope the groom was jerking. I forgot myself, lost control, and by force of old habit neighed and took off at a trot—but my neighing sounded sad, ridiculous, absurd. The herd did not laugh at me—but I noticed that many of them turned away, politely. I imagine they felt disgust and pity and shame; above all, they must have found me ridiculous. Yes, ridiculous—with my thin, inexpressive neck, my big head (I had lost weight by then), my long, clumsy legs and my foolish gait as I trotted, out of habit, round the groom. No one responded to my neighing. They all turned away from me. And suddenly I understood everything—I understood how far removed I was from them, forever—and I don't remember how I made it home with the groom.

I had already shown an inclination to seriousness and deep thinking, but now my character took a decided turn. My spots, which had aroused such incomprehensible contempt in people, my unexpected, unthinkable misfortune, as well as my peculiar position at the stud farm, which I felt but could not yet explain, caused me to withdraw further into myself. I pondered the injustice of humans, who condemned me for being born piebald. I pondered the inconstancy of a mother's love, of woman's love in general, and of its dependence on physical conditions. And, most importantly, I pondered the characteristics of that strange breed of animal with whom we are so closely bound and whom we call humans—the very characteristics that determined my peculiar position at the farm, which I felt but could not understand. The significance of my peculiarity, and of the human characteristics that gave rise to it, was revealed to me by the following events.

It happened in winter, during the holidays. I hadn't been fed or watered all day. The groom, I learnt later, had got drunk. At some point the stable master visited my stall, saw that I had no food and began to curse the missing groom in the foulest of terms. Then he left. The next day that groom came to feed us, together with another one, and I noticed that he looked especially pale and sad; there was, in particular, something striking about the way he moved his long back. It made me feel for him.

He was angrily throwing hay over the lattice and I tried to lay my head across his shoulder—but he punched me on the nose. The blow was so painful that I jumped back. And then he kicked me in the belly with his boot.

"If it hadna been for this mangy bastard," he said, "none of it woulda happened."

"Whatcha mean?" the other groom asked.

"He don't go checkin' on the count's horses, but he sure as hell checks on his own colt, least twice a day."

"What, they gave 'im the piebald?" the other one asked.

"Sold, gave, who the hell knows?... All's I know is I coulda starved the count's horses for all he cares, but if his colt should go without food... 'Lie down,' he says, 'and I'll give you a whippin' you'll never forget.' I tell ya, there's no Christianity in 'im. That heathen cares more for a beast than he does for a man... Counted the lashes 'imself! I bet he ain't got a cross on 'im. The count never whipped me like that—striped my whole back. He ain't got a Christian soul, I tell ya."

What they said about flogging and Christianity was easy enough to grasp, but I was completely in the dark as to the meaning of "*his* colt"—"*his own*". These words indicated that people saw some sort of connection between myself and the stable master. At that time I simply could not understand what this connection might be. Only much later, when I was separated from other horses, did I finally realize what it was. But back then I just couldn't comprehend what it meant to say that *I* was the personal property of a human. The words "my horse" in reference to me, a living horse, seemed as strange as the words "my land" "my air" or "my water".

Yet this left a lasting impression on me. I kept thinking and thinking, and only after long and varied relations with people did I finally grasp the meaning they attributed to these strange words. You see, in life, people are guided not by deeds but by words. They take less pleasure in the opportunity to do or not to do something than they do in the opportunity to apply certain words on which they've agreed to this or that object. These words, which they deem to be very important, are "my" and "mine", and they apply them to all sorts of objects and creatures, and even to land, other people, horses. They agree among themselves that only one person has the right to call any single object "mine". And the person, in this game of theirs, who calls the greatest number of objects "mine" is considered the happiest. Why this is so I cannot say—but it is so. For a long time I tried to explain it to myself, thinking they might derive some direct advantage from all this. It turns out they don't.

For example, many of the people who claimed that I was "their own" horse never rode me. Other people did that. Nor did these so-called owners of mine ever feed me. That too was done by other people. Again, the people who treated me kindly were never my owners: they were coachmen, farriers, total strangers. And the more I observed, the more convinced I became that this went beyond us horses—that the concept of "mine" in general had no other basis than the low, beastly human instinct they call the sense or right of property. A man calls it "my house" but he never lives in it, only busies himself with its construction and upkeep. A merchant calls it "my shop"—say, "my cloth shop"—but he doesn't wear clothes made from the best cloth in the shop. There are people who call land "their own", when they have neither seen that land nor set foot on it. There are people who call other people "their own", when they have never laid eyes on these people—and when their whole relationship to these people consists in doing them harm. There are men who call women "their" women or "their" wives, when these women live with other men. Yes, in life, people aspire not to do what they think good and right, but to label as many objects as possible "their own". I am now convinced that this is the essential difference between people and us. Setting aside all our other superior traits, this alone places us above humans on the ladder of living beings. People—at least those I have known—are guided by words, while we are guided by deeds. Yes, the stable master received the right to call me "his" horse, and this is why he flogged the groom. This realization struck me deeply, and along with the ideas and judgements that my piebald colour aroused in people and the pensiveness into which I was plunged by Mother's betrayal, it made me the serious, deep-thinking gelding that I am.

I was unlucky thrice over: I was piebald, I was a gelding and people imagined that I did not belong to God and to myself, as is natural to all living beings, but that I belonged to the stable master.

And these imaginings of theirs had many consequences. First of all, I was kept apart from the herd, was better fed, was lunged more frequently and was harnessed earlier than the others—in my third year. I remember how the stable master, who imagined that I belonged to him, came to harness me with a crowd of grooms, expecting me to buck and resist. They pulled back my upper lip with one rope and wound more ropes all around me to lead me into the shafts. Then they put a cross of wide belts on my back and tied them to the shafts, to keep me from kicking—when all I had wanted, the whole time, was an opportunity to demonstrate my eagerness and love of work.

They were surprised that I took to all this like a seasoned horse. They began to exercise me and I practised trotting. I got better and better by the day, so that after three months the count himself, and many others besides, were praising my pace. But it's a strange thing—precisely because they imagined that I was not their own, but belonged instead to the stable master, my pace took on a different meaning for them.

The stallions—my brothers—were raced, measured, timed. People went out to look at them, hitched them to gilded carts, covered them with expensive horse cloths. I was hitched to a plain cart and took the stable master on his rounds to visit Chesmenka and other farms. All this was due to my being piebald—and above all to my being the property, in human opinion, not of the count but of the stable master.

Tomorrow, if we live that long, I will tell you of the most important consequence that the stable master's supposed right of property had for me.

—

That whole day the horses treated Pace-setter with great respect, while Nester was as rude as usual. At one point the peasant's little roan horse came close to the herd and resumed his neighing, and the chestnut filly resumed her flirting.

## VII

## *Third Night*

A new moon arose. Its slender crescent illuminated the figure of Pace-setter standing in the middle of the yard. The other horses crowded around him.

—

THE MOST IMPORTANT, most surprising consequence of the fact that I belonged not to the count, not to God, but to the stable master, was that the very thing that constitutes our chief merit—a quick pace—became the cause of my exile. They were racing Swan in circles, and the stable master, returning from Chesmenka, pulled me up to the track and stopped. Swan went past. He ran well enough but I knew he was showing off—he didn't have the kind of efficiency I had developed, so that as soon as one of my hooves touched the ground another would be lifted, not a single exertion going to waste, every movement pushing forward. Swan went past. I pulled towards the track and the stable master didn't hold me back. "Hell, why not give my pinto a try?" he shouted, and when Swan came abreast of us again, he let me go. Swan was already at full speed, so I was behind in the first round, but in the second I began to gain on him, then pulled close to his cart, drew level and pulled ahead. They raced us again—same result. I was the faster horse. And this horrified everyone. They decided to sell me off as soon as possible and never mention me again. "If the count finds out about this," they said, "there'll be hell to pay!" And so they sold me to a horse-trader in Korennaya. I didn't stay with the horse-trader long. He sold me to a hussar who came to buy remounts. It was all so unfair, so cruel, that I was glad when I was taken away from Khrenovoye, separated forever from everything that had been near and dear to me. Life among the other horses had been too painful for me. They could look forward to love, honour, freedom, while I—all I could expect was work and humiliation, humiliation and work, until the end of my days... And why was that? Because I had been born piebald—and on account of my colour I was forced to become someone's property.

—

Pace-setter could say no more that evening. Something occurred to alarm the horses. Merchant's Wife, a mare due to foal, who had at first been listening to the story, suddenly turned away and slowly hobbled into a shed, where she began to groan so loudly that the others could not ignore her. She lay down, then got up again, then lay back down. The old brood mares understood right away what was happening to her, but the younger horses grew agitated, left the gelding and surrounded the sufferer. By morning there was a new foal, unsteady on its legs. Nester shouted to the groom, the mare and foal were led into a stall, and the herd was driven out without them.

## VIII

### Fourth Night

In the evening, after the gate was closed and everything grew quiet, the piebald went on with his story.

———

I HAVE MANAGED to make many observations of people and horses as I passed from hand to hand, again and again. I stayed the longest with two masters: the prince— that hussar officer I'd mentioned—and an old woman who lived by the Church of St Nicholas the Wonderworker.

The time I spent with the hussar officer was the happiest of my life.

Although he brought about my ruin, although he never loved anything or anyone, I myself loved him and continue to love him for that very reason. Yes, that is precisely what I liked in him—that he was handsome, happy and rich, and for this reason did not love anyone. You know that exalted equine feeling... His coldness, his cruelty and my complete dependence on him lent a special intensity to my love. *Kill me*, I thought when the times were good, *ride me till I break down—and I will be all the happier.*

He bought me from the horse-trader to whom the stable master had sold me for eight hundred roubles. He bought me because no one else had a piebald horse. This was the best time of my life. He had a mistress. I knew this because I took him to see her every day, and took her to see him, and sometimes took them both out. His mistress was beautiful, he was beautiful, even his coachman was beautiful—and I loved them all for their beauty. Yes, life was a pleasure then. In the morning the groom would come to brush me—not the coachman himself, but the groom. He was a young fellow, this groom, one of the peasants. He'd open the door, let out the steam we'd built up in the night, pitch out the manure, take off our horse cloths and begin to fuss over our bodies with his brush, laying whitish strips of dandruff from his curry comb on the battered floorboards. I'd playfully nip at his sleeve and tap my foot. Then we'd be led, one by one, to a trough of cold water, and the young fellow would gaze admiringly at my smooth spotted coat—the work of his hands—my legs straight as arrows, my large hooves, my glossy croup and my back, broad enough to sleep on. Tall racks would be stuffed with hay, oak mangers filled with oats. And then Feofan, the coachman, would come in.

Coachman and master had much in common. Neither of them feared a thing and neither loved anyone, and for this they were both beloved. Feofan went about in a red shirt, plush trousers and a long coat. I liked it when, on a holiday, he'd strut into the stable in his long coat, his hair all pomaded, and shout, "Whatsamatter, ya dumb nag? Forgot, eh?" And then he'd prod me in the thigh with the handle of the pitchfork—never so hard that it hurt, just as a joke. And I'd get the joke right away, pin back an ear and snap my teeth.

We had a black stallion, one of a pair. I'd be harnessed with him at night. Centaur was his name—never could take a joke, always angry as the devil. We were put in neighbouring stalls and there were times when we took serious bites at each other. But Feofan was never afraid of him. He'd come right up and shout—and Centaur, he'd be ready to kill—but no: Feofan would slip on the halter. One time Centaur and I took off down Kuznetsky Bridge Street. Neither the master nor the coachman took fright—both just laughed and shouted at people, reined us back and turned so that we didn't run anyone over.

In their service I lost my finest attributes and half my life. They let me drink too much water, spoilt my legs. And yet these were the best years of my life. At noon they would come and harness me, black my hooves, moisten my forelock and mane, and lead me into the shafts.

The sledge was made of wicker and draped in velvet, the harness had little silver buckles, the reins were of silk, and for a time I wore fine blue netting. Yes, when all the belts and straps were fitted and fastened, it was impossible to tell where the harness ended and the horse began. I was harnessed in the stable, on a tether. Then Feofan would strut in, his backside wider than his shoulders, a crimson sash as high up as his armpits. He'd examine the harness, take his seat in the sledge, straighten his coat, put his foot in the stirrup, crack a joke, hang his whip over his shoulder—just for the sake of appearances, mind you, as he almost never hit me—and say: "Walk!" And I'd move through the gate, relishing each step, and the cook who'd come out to dump the slops would stop on the threshold, and the peasants carting firewood back to the yard would stare at us, eyes bulging. We'd ride out a little way, then stop. Then the footmen would come, coachmen would drive up and they'd all start talking with Feofan. And everyone would wait. There were days when we'd stand at the entrance for three hours or more—moving forward a bit, then turning back and stopping again.

At last there'd be a bustle in the doorway and paunchy, grey-headed Tikhon would come out in his tailcoat. "Here!" he'd shout. In those days, there was none of this silly "Forward!" business—as if I don't know to move forward, not backwards. Feofan would give a click, we'd drive up to the house and then the prince would hurry out, not a care in the world, as if there were nothing at all special about this sledge, this horse or Feofan, who'd be bending his back and stretching out his arms in a posture that looked impossible to hold for long. Yes, the prince would come out wearing a shako and an overcoat with a grey beaver collar that hid his ruddy, black-browed, beautiful face—a face that should never be hidden. He'd come out, stepping briskly across the carpet—his sabre, spurs and copper heels jangling—as if he were in a great hurry, paying no attention to Feofan and me, whom everyone except him was watching and admiring. Feofan would give another click, I'd lean into the reins and, steadily, at a walking pace, we'd drive right up to the prince. I'd cast a glance at him and throw up my thoroughbred head with its fine forelock. The prince, in high spirits, might joke with Feofan, who'd respond, just barely turning his beautiful head, and, without lowering his arms, move the reins with a barely noticeable gesture, which I would fully understand—and clop, clop, clop, with ever-widening strides, with every muscle quivering, kicking back dirty snow at the front of the sledge, I was off. Back then, too, there was none of this foolishness, with the coachman shouting, "Oh!" as if he were in pain. No, Feofan would shout the unintelligible, "Get along! Watch it!" Yes, he'd shout, "Get along! Watch it!" And people would make way, and stop, and crane their necks to get a glimpse at the fine-looking gelding, the fine-looking coachman and the fine-looking gentleman.

I loved to overtake trotters. I loved it when Feofan and I would spot, from afar, a competitor worthy of our efforts and would fly like the wind, gradually rolling closer and closer—with me kicking dirt all the way to the back of the sledge, drawing level with the passenger and snorting above his head, drawing level with the harness saddle, then with the shaft bow, until I don't see the horse any more, only hear the sound of him fading far behind. And the prince, Feofan and I, we don't say a word. We pretend that we're just going about our business, that we don't even notice those who happen to cross our path on inferior horses. Yes, I loved to overtake them—but I also loved to meet a good trotter: a moment, a sound, a glance, and we've already parted, flying alone again, each in his own direction.

—

The horses heard the gate creak and the voices of Nester and Vaska.

## Fifth Night

The weather had begun to change. Since early morning the sky had been overcast and there was no dew, but it was warm and the mosquitoes were biting. As soon as the horses were driven back into the yard they gathered around the gelding and he finished his story:

———

MY HAPPY LIFE soon came to an end. It lasted only two years. The happiest moment came at the end of the second winter, followed by the greatest misfortune. This happened at Shrovetide. I took the prince to the races. Satin and Bull were running. I don't know what the prince was doing in the pavilion, but I know that he came out and ordered Feofan to drive onto the track. I remember I was placed on the track, with Satin beside me. Satin had an outrider—and me? Still pulling my sledge, I overtook him at the turn. Such laughter, roars of delight…

When I was cooling down afterwards a crowd walked along behind me. At least five people offered to buy me for thousands of roubles but the prince just laughed, showing off his white teeth.

"Not a chance," he said. "This isn't a horse, it's a friend. I wouldn't trade him for a mountain of gold. Farewell, gentlemen." And he got into the sledge.

"Ostozhenka!" This was the street where his mistress lived. And we were off. Yes, that was our last happy day.

We reached her apartment. He called her "his" but she fell in love with another man and ran away. The prince found out about this at her apartment. It was five o'clock; without unharnessing me, he took off after her. They did something they'd never done before—they whipped me, forcing me to gallop. For the first time in my life I made a false step—I felt so ashamed, wanted to correct it—but suddenly I heard the prince shout in a strange voice: "Faster!" The whip whistled and cut into my back—and I galloped, my back legs beating against the iron front of the sledge. We caught up with her after sixteen miles. I got him where he wanted to go, but all that night I kept shivering and couldn't eat a thing. The next morning they gave me water. I drank it—and I was never the same horse again. I was ill. They began maiming, torturing me—"treating" me, as people call it. My hoofs fell off, my joints swelled and my legs grew bent; my chest was thin and I grew listless, weak all over. They sold me off to a horse-trader. He fed me on carrots and I don't know what else, and he turned me into something that was no longer me but that might fool the ignorant. I had no strength left, no speed. What's more, whenever there was a buyer, the trader would come into my stall and torment me, scaring and lashing me with his whip—which hurt so badly—working me up into a frenzy; then he would rub down my welts and lead me out. An old woman bought me. She would always drive to St Nicholas the Wonderworker and she would have her coachman flogged. He used to cry in my stall. And that's when I learnt that tears have a pleasant flavour, salty. Then the old woman died. Her steward took me to the countryside and sold me to a pedlar. I ate too much wheat and grew ill again, worse than before. Then I was sold to a peasant. With him I ploughed, and ate almost nothing. A ploughshare cut my leg. Then I grew ill again. The peasant traded me off to a gypsy. The gypsy tortured me terribly, then finally sold me to the steward of this place. So here I am.

—

All were silent. A drizzling rain began to fall.

## IX

Returning home the following evening, the herd happened to see their master, who had a guest. As she approached the house, Zhuldyba glanced sidelong at the two male figures: one was the young master in his straw hat, the other a tall, fat, flabby military man. The old mare glanced sidelong, then veered towards the guest. The younger horses hesitated and grew flustered, especially when the master and his guest began to walk among them, talking and pointing.

"That one there, the dapple grey, I bought from Voeikov," said the master.

"And what about this one here—the young black mare with the white legs? She's a fine one," said the guest.

They examined a great many horses, running after and stopping them, one by one. The chestnut filly drew their attention.

"That one I kept from the Khrenovoye riding horse breed," the master said.

It was impossible to examine all the horses in passing. The master hollered to Nester and the old man trotted over, hurriedly tapping his heels against the gelding's side. The gelding limped on one foot but he still ran—he ran in such a way that it was clear he would never grumble, even if he were made to run this way to the very ends of the earth, until his strength gave out. He was even ready to gallop, and he gave it a try with his right foot.

"I can tell you right now that there's no better horse in all of Russia," said the master, pointing to one of the mares. The guest offered his praise. The master was excited; he walked around, ran after his horses, showed them off and told the guest about each animal's history and breed. Although the guest seemed to find all this talk terribly boring, he kept thinking up questions so as to appear interested.

"Yes, yes," he kept saying, absently.

"Take a look," said the master, responding to nothing the guest had said. "Take a look at those legs... She sure cost me plenty, but she's given me three trotters already."

"Good foals, eh?" asked the guest.

And so they looked over nearly all the horses, until there was nothing more to show. They fell silent.

"Well? Shall we go?"

"Yes, let's."

They went towards the gate. The guest was glad that the demonstration was over and that they would now go back to the house, where he could eat, drink, have a smoke; he cheered up visibly. Walking past Nester—who sat on the piebald gelding, awaiting further orders—the guest slapped the gelding on the croup with his big fat hand.

"This fella's painted all over!" he said. "Had one just like him—I told you, remember?"

The master realized that the subject was not one of his own horses and stopped listening; he kept turning his head, admiring his herd.

All of a sudden, a foolish, feeble, senile neigh sounded at his side, right above his ear. It was the gelding; he had begun to neigh, but then, as if embarrassed, broke off. Neither the guest nor the master paid any attention to the sound and went back towards the house. Pace-setter had recognized that flabby old man: it was his beloved master, the once dazzling, rich and beautiful Serpukhovskoy.

X

The drizzle continued. The stable yard was cold and damp, but in the master's house things were different. There, in the luxurious drawing room, at a table laid for a luxurious evening tea, sat the host, the hostess and their guest.

The hostess, who sat by the samovar, was pregnant—very noticeably so, thanks to her puffed-out belly, her strained, straight-backed posture, her plumpness and particularly her large eyes, which looked inwards, meekly and significantly.

The host was holding a box of ten-year-old cigars—very special, of a sort no one else had, he insisted—and was getting ready to boast about them to his guest. He was a handsome man of twenty-five, fresh, sleek and well groomed. At home he wore a new, thick, loose-footing two-piece suit, made in London. Big expensive charms dangled from his watch chain. The cufflinks on his shirt were also massive: gold with turquoise. He had a tuft of beard à la Napoleon III, and his pomaded and pointed moustaches stuck out in a manner that could only have been fashioned in Paris. The hostess wore a silk muslin dress patterned with large, colourful flowers, and large golden pins of some special design adorned the thick, dark-blonde hair on her head—hair that was beautiful, though not entirely her own. On her hands was a multitude of bracelets and rings, all expensive. The samovar was of silver, the service of the finest china. The footman—magnificent in his tailcoat, white vest and tie—stood by the door like a statue, awaiting orders. The bentwood furniture was elaborately curved and brightly upholstered; the dark wallpaper was decorated with large flowers. Around the table, tinkling the little bells on its silver collar, moved an unusually exquisite Italian greyhound, whose unusually difficult English name its owners could never pronounce, as neither spoke English. In the corner, amid plants and flowers, stood an inlaid piano. Everything exuded an air of novelty, luxury and rarity. Everything was fine, very fine, but it all bore a definite stamp of excess, of wealth and of a total absence of intellectual interests.

The host, a strong, sanguine fellow who loved a trotting race, was of a breed that will never die out— fellows that drive about in sable coats, toss expensive bouquets to actresses, drink the most expensive, most fashionable wines in the most expensive hotels, hand out prizes that bear their own names and keep the most expensive mistresses.

Their guest, Nikita Serpukhovskoy, was over forty, tall, fat, bald-pated, with bushy moustaches and whiskers. It was clear that he had been handsome in his youth but now he had declined—physically, morally, financially.

He was so deep in debt that he had to serve the government just to avoid prison, and he was now on his way to a provincial town to become the head of a stud farm—a position secured for him by highly placed relatives. He wore a military tunic and blue trousers. These were of a sort that only a rich man would have made for himself, as were his undergarments. His watch, too, was English. And his boots had wonderful soles, as thick as a finger.

Nikita Serpukhovskoy had managed to squander two million roubles over the course of his life, and now owed a hundred and twenty thousand. A fortune of that size always gives one a push forward, allowing one to live on credit, almost luxuriously, for a good ten years after it's gone. Now those ten years were coming to an end, the push was almost spent, and Nikita's life was turning bitter. He had begun to drink—that is, to get drunk; this was new for him, although, properly speaking, he never actually began or stopped drinking. But the clearest signs of his descent were the restlessness of his glances (his eyes had become shifty) and the unsteadiness of his voice and gestures. This restlessness was so striking because it had obviously taken hold of him quite recently; one could see that he had never, in all his life, been afraid of anything or anyone, and that this new fear, so alien to his nature, had come to him only now, after great suffering. The host and hostess noticed this and exchanged knowing glances that showed they were only postponing a detailed discussion of the subject until bedtime, and were tolerating poor Nikita, even taking care of him. The sight of his young host's happiness humiliated Nikita, reminding him of his own irrevocable past and inspiring painful envy.

"Don't mind my smoking, do you, Marie?" he asked his hostess in that special, subtle tone that comes only with experience—the polite and friendly yet not entirely respectful tone that worldly men take with kept women, as opposed to wives. Not that he meant to insult her; on the contrary, if anything he was eager to win both her and her keeper's favour, although he would never admit this to himself. But he had grown used to speaking in this way to women of her sort. He knew that she herself would have been surprised, even offended, if he were to treat her like a lady. And besides, he had to reserve a special tone of deference for the actual wife of his equal. He always treated women of her sort with respect, not because he shared the so-called convictions propagated by the intellectual journals (he never read that rubbish) concerning the respect due to every individual, the senselessness of marriage, etc., but simply because this was how decent people behaved, and he was a decent, though fallen, man.

He took a cigar. But then the host awkwardly picked up a whole handful of cigars and offered them to his guest.

"They're very good—you'll see. Take them."

Nikita waved away the offer, and his eyes glimmered with a flash of shame and offence.

"Thank you." He took out his own cigar case. "Try one of mine."

The sensitive hostess noticed this and hurried to distract his attention.

"I love cigars, I really do. I would smoke them myself if I weren't already surrounded by smokers."

And she smiled her kind, beautiful smile. He smiled back at her, unsteadily. Two of his teeth were gone.

"No, take this one," the insensitive host persisted. "They aren't as strong. Fritz, *bringen Sie noch eine Kasten*," he said, "*dedort zwei*."[3]

The German footman brought another box.

"What kind do you like? The strong ones? Here, these are excellent. Take them all." He kept on shoving cigars at his guest, obviously glad to have someone to boast to of his rare possessions, and oblivious to everything else. Serpukhovskoy lit up and hurried to continue the conversation they had started.

"So how much did Satin cost you?" he asked.

"A tidy sum, no less than five thousand. But I've already made it back. I tell you, the colts he gave me!"

"Trotters?" asked Serpukhovskoy.

"Excellent trotters. His son took three prizes this year—in Tula, in Moscow and in Petersburg—racing against Voeikov's Raven. His rider, the scoundrel, let him make four false steps, otherwise he would have left Raven behind the flag."

"He's still a little green. And too much Dutch in him, I say," Serpukhovskoy remarked.

"Well, that's what mares are for! I'll show you tomorrow. Bought Goody for three thousand, Sweety for two."

And the host again began to enumerate his wealth. The hostess saw that this was hard for Serpukhovskoy to take, that he was only pretending to listen.

"Would you like some more tea?" she asked.

"No," replied the host, and went on talking. She rose. He stopped her, embraced her and kissed her.

Serpukhovskoy smiled an unnatural smile, at them and for them, but when the host rose, embraced the hostess and disappeared behind the door-curtain, his expression suddenly changed. He heaved a heavy sigh and a look of despair settled on his flabby face—a look of despair and even of malice.

## XI

The host returned and sat down across from Nikita, smiling. For a while neither of them spoke.

"You were saying… You bought from Voeikov…" said Serpukhovskoy, feigning nonchalance.

"Yes, yes, Satin. I told you. I wanted to buy some mares from Dubovitsky, but the ones he had left were rubbish."

"He's down and out," said Serpukhovskoy, and suddenly stopped and glanced around. He remembered that he owed this down-and-outer twenty thousand. And if anyone could be called "down and out", it was certainly himself. He fell silent.

Again, for a long time, neither man said a word. The host was searching for something else he could boast about to his guest. Serpukhovskoy was searching for some way to show that he did not consider himself down and out. But their brains worked slowly, despite efforts to enliven them with cigars. *Isn't it time for a drink?* thought Serpukhovskoy. *I've got to have a drink or he'll bore me to death*, thought the host.

"So, how long are you here for?" asked Serpukhovskoy.

"Oh, another month or so. Well, shall we dine? Fritz, is it ready?"

They went into the dining room. There, beneath a hanging lamp, stood a table laden with candles and an assortment of the most uncommon things: siphons, little dolls on stoppers, uncommon wine in decanters, uncommon appetizers, all kinds of liquors. They drank, ate, drank some more, ate some more, and the conversation finally came to life. Serpukhovskoy grew flushed and began to speak freely.

They talked about women, about who kept which kind: a gypsy, a dancer, a Frenchwoman.

"Well, have you left Mathieu?" asked the host. This was the kept woman who had ruined Serpukhovskoy.

"No, she left me. Brother, I tell you, when I look back on all the things I've lost in my life... These days I'm glad when I manage to round up a thousand roubles. I'm glad when I manage to get away from everyone. I can't stand Moscow. Oh, what's the use in talking about it?..."

The host was bored. He wanted to talk about himself—to boast. But all Serpukhovskoy wanted to talk about was his own life—his brilliant past. The host refilled his guest's wine glass and waited for him to finish so that he could finally talk about himself. He wanted to tell him about his stud farm, which was set up better than any other had ever been, and about his Marie, who loved him with all her heart, not only for his money.

"About my stud farm, I wanted to tell you that—" he began. But Serpukhovskoy interrupted him.

"There was a time," he said, "when I loved the good life, and knew how to live it. You tell me about riding—well, what's the fastest horse you've got?"

The host was delighted to have the chance to say more about his stud farm, and so he began to answer—but Serpukhovskoy interrupted him again.

"Yes, yes," he said. "But with you breeders, it's all for the sake of vanity—it isn't for pleasure, for life. I was different. I was telling you earlier that I had a riding horse, a piebald, just like the one your herdsman rides, same spots. Now that was a horse! You couldn't have known… This was back in 1842. I had just come to Moscow and I went to a horse-trader and saw him—a piebald gelding. Well put together. I liked him. The price? A thousand. Well, I liked him, so I bought him and drove him. I never had such a horse—and you haven't either, and you never will. I've never seen a better trotter, a stronger, more beautiful horse. You were just a boy then, you couldn't have known, but I bet you heard of him. He was famous all over Moscow."

"Yes, I heard of him," the host responded reluctantly. "But I wanted to tell you about mine—"

"So you heard, then. I bought him just like that—no pedigree, no certificate. Later, Voeikov and I found out the truth. He'd been sired by Gracious I. Pace-setter, they called him, on account of his measured stride. Because he was piebald, they kept him out of the stud at Khrenovoye and gave him to the stable master, who had him castrated and sold him off to the horse-trader. Ah, my friend, they don't make them like that any more! Those were the days... 'When we were young!'" he sang the refrain of the gypsy ballad. The wine was getting to him. "Yes, it was a fine time. I was twenty-five and earning eighty thousand silver roubles a year. Not a single grey hair on my head, teeth like pearls. Whatever I tried, it all came out right—and then it was all over."

"But they weren't as fast back then," said the host, taking advantage of the pause. "I tell you, my first horses began to walk without—"

"Your horses? Trust me, ours were faster."

"What do you mean they were faster?"

"I mean they were faster. Listen, I remember as if it were yesterday. Once I drove out to the races in Moscow. None of my horses were running. I didn't much like trotters. I kept thoroughbreds—General, Cholet, Mohammed. I had my piebald gelding in harness. My driver was a nice fellow—I loved him, but he's a drunk now. So I drive up and hear, 'Serpukhovskoy, when will you get yourself some trotters?' And I say, 'I don't need your damn peasant trotters! My piebald hack can outrun them all.' And they say, 'No he won't.' So I say, 'Bet you a thousand.' We shake on it—and the horses are off and running. Well, mine comes in five seconds ahead, wins a thousand. That's nothing! Why, one time, I covered sixty-six miles on three thoroughbreds in three hours. All Moscow knows about that."

And Serpukhovskoy began to lie so smoothly and continuously that the host could not get a word in edgewise. He sat opposite his guest, looking glum, and kept filling their glasses with wine just to keep busy.

They were still sitting there as dawn broke. The host was bored to tears. He got up.

"Well, if it's time for bed…" said Serpukhovskoy, rising to his feet and staggering a bit. Then he went off to the room set aside for him, panting all the way.

The host was in bed with his mistress.

"He's completely unbearable. Drunk out of his mind and lying without stop."

"And he keeps making eyes at me."

"I'm afraid he'll ask me for money."

Serpukhovskoy lay in bed with his clothes on, panting.

*Lied through my teeth*, he thought. *Doesn't matter. The wine was good, and he's a rotten pig. A common merchant. I'm a rotten pig, too*, he thought and laughed. *I used to keep women, now I'm a kept man. Yes, that Winkler dame will support me. I'll take her money. Serves him right, serves him right... Just need to undress... Boots won't come off...*

"Hey!" he shouted, but the man assigned to help him had gone off to sleep long ago.

He sat down, took off his tunic and waistcoat, and somehow managed to wriggle out of his trousers, but for a long time he could not pull off his boots; his soft belly kept getting in the way. He finally got one of them off, but after struggling and struggling with the other he tired himself out and gave up. And so, with his foot still stuck in the bootleg, he fell back on the bed and began to snore, filling the room with the stench of tobacco, wine and dirty old age.

## XII

If memories returned to Pace-setter's mind that night, they were driven away by Vaska. The lad threw a rug over him and galloped off to the tavern, where he kept him tethered by the door, next to a peasant's horse, until dawn. The two horses licked each other. In the morning, when the gelding went back to the herd, he kept rubbing himself.

*Awfully itchy*, he thought. *Hurts.*

Five days passed. They called in a farrier. He happily declared, "Scabies. Let me sell 'im to the gypsies."

"What for? Cut his throat and be done with it."

The morning was still and clear. The herd was taken out to pasture but Pace-setter stayed behind. A strange man appeared—thin, dark, dirty, his caftan bespattered with something black. This was the flayer. Without looking at Pace-setter he took hold of his halter and led him away. Pace-setter went quietly, never glancing back and dragging his legs as usual, his hind feet catching in the straw. After stepping through the gate he pulled towards the well, but the flayer jerked him back and said, "No use now."

The flayer and Vaska, who was walking behind him, came to a hollow behind the brick shed and stopped, as if there were something special about this very ordinary spot. Handing the halter to Vaska, the flayer removed his caftan, rolled up his sleeves, took a knife and whetstone from his bootleg, and began to sharpen the knife. The gelding reached for the halter, wanting to chew it a bit out of boredom, but it was too far away; he sighed and closed his eyes. His lower lip sagged, revealing his ground-down yellow teeth, and he dozed off to the sound of the knife being sharpened. Only his aching, swollen, outstretched leg kept twitching. Suddenly he felt someone's hand on his throat, lifting up his head. He opened his eyes. There were two dogs in front of him. One was sniffing at the flayer, while the other sat and gazed at the gelding, as if expecting something from him. The gelding glanced at them and began to rub his jaw against the hand that held him.

*Want to treat me*, he thought. *Well, let them.*

And he did indeed feel that something was done to his throat. It hurt. He started, stamped his foot, but restrained himself and waited for what would come next. What came next was liquid, pouring in a thick stream down his neck and chest. He sighed profoundly, his sides heaving. And he felt much better. The whole burden of his life felt lighter. He closed his eyes and began to lower his head—no one was holding it up any longer. Then his neck began to bend, his legs trembled and his entire body swayed. He was not so much frightened as surprised. It was all so new. He was surprised, and he rushed ahead, upwards—but his hind legs got tangled and he reeled sideways. Trying to find a footing with his front legs, he fell forward and onto his left side. The flayer waited until the convulsions had stopped and chased away the dogs, who had been creeping closer; then he grabbed a leg, turned the gelding onto his back, told Vaska to hold the animal still and began to flay it.

"Was a real horse, too," said Vaska.

"It it hada been better fed, skin woulda been good," said the flayer.

The herd was returning home that evening, going downhill, and those who walked on the left saw something red down below; dogs fussed around it busily, and crows and kites hovered overhead. One of the dogs, its paws pressed against the carrion, shook its head from side to side and tore off, with a cracking noise, what it had seized in its teeth. The chestnut filly halted, stretched out her head and neck, and stood sniffing the air for a long time. They barely managed to drive her onwards.

At dawn, in the old forest, in a clearing at the overgrown bottom of a ravine, big-headed wolf cubs were howling with joy. There were five of them; four were nearly equal in size, while the fifth was small, its head larger than its body. A lean, moulting she-wolf crawled out of the bushes, dragging her full belly with saggy teats along the ground, and sat down opposite the cubs, who formed a semicircle before her. She walked over to the smallest one, lowered her tail and pointed her muzzle downwards, made several convulsive movements, opened her sharp-toothed mouth and, straining, disgorged a large chunk of horsemeat. The bigger cubs scampered towards her, but she scared them back and let the little one have the whole chunk. Snarling as if he were angry, he pulled the horsemeat under him and began to eat. The she-wolf then disgorged for the second cub, for the third, for all five, and finally lay down in front of them to rest.

A week later only a huge skull and two big bones lay near the brick shed. Everything else had been dragged away. Towards summer a bone-grubbing peasant came by and took these too, so as to put them into use.

The dead body of Serpukhovskoy, which had walked the earth, eating and drinking, was placed in the ground much later. Neither his skin, nor his meat, nor his bones proved to be of any use whatsoever. And just as his dead body, walking the earth, had been a great burden to everyone for a full twenty years, so too did its placement in the ground turn out to be simply another encumbrance for people.

For a long time no one had needed him. For a long time he had been nothing but a burden. Nevertheless, the dead who bury their dead found it necessary to dress this bloated, already rotting body in a good uniform and good boots, to lay it in a good new coffin with new tassels on its four corners, to put this new coffin in another one made of lead, and to bring it to Moscow, where they would dig up some long-buried human bones and, in that very spot, hide this rotting, worm-infested body in its new uniform and polished boots, covering it up with earth.

# THREE DEATHS

I T WAS AUTUMN. Two carriages were rolling along the high road at a quick trot. The first was occupied by two women. One of these was the mistress, thin and pale, the other her plumpish, lustrously ruddy maid. Strands of hair, short and dry, occasionally escaped from under the maid's faded cap, and a red hand in a torn glove would shoot up to tuck them out of sight. Her high bosom was covered by a brightly coloured shawl and radiated health; her quick black eyes now watched the fields flying past the window, now glanced timidly at her mistress, now peered restlessly into every corner of the carriage. The mistress's hat dangled from the ceiling of the carriage right in front of the maid's nose; a puppy lay on her lap; her feet bounced up from the boxes on the floor and drummed against them, lightly accompanying the creaking springs and rattling windows.

The mistress sat with her hands folded on her knees and her eyes closed. Rocking weakly against the cushions behind her back and wrinkling her forehead ever so slightly, she tried to suppress her cough. She wore a white nightcap and a blue kerchief tied around her pale, delicate neck. A straight line, disappearing under the cap, parted her fair, remarkably flat pomaded hair, and there was something dry and deathly about the whiteness of the skin that showed in this wide parting. Wilted, yellowish skin was drawn loosely over the fine, beautiful features of her face and grew flushed on the cheeks and cheekbones. Her lips were dry and tense, her sparse eyelashes did not curl, and her cloth travelling dress lay in straight folds over her sunken chest. Although the mistress's eyes were closed, her face expressed weariness, irritation and habitual suffering.

The lackey, reclining on the coachbox, was napping, while the driver shouted briskly at his team of four large, sweaty horses and occasionally looked back at the other driver, who was shouting from the barouche. Smoothly and quickly, the tyres made broad, parallel tracks in the limey mud. The sky was grey and cold, and a damp mist fell on the fields and the road. The carriage was stuffy and smelt of eau de Cologne and dust. The sick woman leant her head back and slowly opened her eyes. They were large and lustrous, of a lovely dark colour.

"Again," she said, and nervously pushed aside the hem of the maid's cloak, which had just barely brushed against her leg, with a beautiful, emaciated hand. Her mouth twisted into an expression of pain. Matryosha lifted the hem of her cloak with both hands, rose up on her strong legs, and sat down further away. Her fresh face blushed brightly. The sick woman's lovely dark eyes greedily followed the maid's every movement. She had put both her hands on the seat and wanted to raise herself as the maid had done, so as to sit up a bit higher, but her strength failed her. Her mouth twisted again and her whole face was distorted with a look of impotent, malignant irony. "You could at least help me… No, don't bother, I can do it myself—just don't put any more of your bags behind me… Will you do me that kindness? No, don't touch anything—you don't know how…" The mistress closed her eyes, then quickly lifted her eyelids again and looked at the maid. Matryosha was gazing at her, biting her red lower lip. A heavy sigh rose from the sick woman's chest but soon transformed into a fit of coughing. She turned away, grimacing and clutching her chest with both hands. After the fit passed off, she again closed her eyes and sat motionless. The carriage and barouche drove into the village. Matryosha drew a plump hand from under her shawl and crossed herself.

"What is this?" the mistress asked.

"Post station, madam."

"I'm asking why you crossed yourself."

"There's a church, madam."

The sick woman turned to the window and slowly began to cross herself, her large eyes open wide and fixed on the big village church round which the carriage was passing.

They pulled up at the post station. The sick woman's husband and her doctor stepped out of the barouche and approached her carriage.

"How are you feeling?" the doctor asked, feeling her pulse.

"How are you, dear friend? Tired?" the husband asked in French. "Would you like to get out?"

Matryosha gathered her bundles and huddled up in a corner, so as not to interfere.

"I'm fine. No worse than before," the sick woman replied. "I won't join you."

The husband stood there a while, then went into the station house. Matryosha hopped out of the carriage and ran on tiptoe through the dirt towards the gate.

"My being unwell is no reason why you should skip breakfast," the sick woman said, smiling slightly at the doctor, who was standing by the window.

*None of them care about me—not one bit*, she thought to herself as soon as the doctor, after stepping quietly away from the carriage, had trotted up the stairs of the station house. *They're well —that's all they care about. Oh God…*

"Well, Eduard Ivanovich?" the husband greeted the doctor, smiling cheerfully and rubbing his hands. "I've sent someone to fetch my wine from the carriage. What do you think?"

"Not a bad idea," the doctor responded.

"Tell me, how is she?" the husband asked with a sigh, lowering his voice and raising his eyebrows.

"I've already told you. She'll be lucky if she reaches Moscow, God willing, much less Italy. Especially in this weather."

"God… My God… What are we to do?" the husband asked, placing a hand over his eyes. "Over here!" he added, addressing the man with the wine.

"You should have kept her at home," the doctor answered with a shrug.

"But tell me, what was I to do?" the husband objected. "I tried everything to dissuade her—told her that our means were limited, that my affairs would suffer, that our children would miss us… She would hear none of it. She's making plans to live abroad as if she were in perfect health. And to tell her the truth about her condition—why, that would kill her…"

"Vasily Dmitrich, she is already killed. You must accept this. A person can't live without lungs, and lungs don't grow back. It is sad, it is difficult, but what can one do? Our job now is to make her last days as easy as possible. What she really needs is a priest."

"My God… Please understand my position, mentioning her last will… No, I won't do it—no matter what. You know how good, how kind she is…"

"Yes, all the same, do try to persuade her to stay until the winter roads are open," said the doctor, shaking his head significantly. "Nothing good will come of this journey…"

"Aksyusha! Hey, Aksyusha!" the stationmaster's daughter squealed, stamping about on the filthy back porch in her fur-trimmed jacket. "Let's go have a look at the Shirkinsky lady—they say they're takin' her abroad 'cause she's sick in the chest. Ain't never seen a consumptive before."

Aksyusha skipped over the threshold and the two girls dashed out of the gate, clutching each other's hands. Slackening their pace, they walked by the carriage and peered in at the open window. The sick woman turned her head towards them, but then perceived their curiosity, knit her brows and turned away.

"Heavens above!" said the stationmaster's daughter, quickly shaking her head. "What a beauty she was—and look at her now. Enough to scare you, isn't it? Did you get a good look, Aksyusha?"

"I did—and how skinny she is!" Aksyusha nodded along. "Let's go and have another look—we'll make as if we're heading to the well. She turned away, but I still saw her… Masha, it's pitiful, ain't it?"

"Oh, this mud's something awful!" Masha answered, and both girls raced back through the gate.

*I must look a fright*, thought the sick woman. *We have to hurry, hurry abroad, and I'll get better, be myself again.*

"Well, how are you, my friend?" asked her husband as he approached the carriage, still chewing the last of his food.

*Always the same question*, the sick woman thought. *And he's eating!*

"Fine," she muttered through her teeth.

"You know, my friend, I'm afraid the journey, in this weather, will injure your health and Eduard Ivanovich feels the same way. Shouldn't we turn back?"

She remained angrily silent.

"The weather might improve, they'll restore the roads and you might feel better—we'd all go together."

"Excuse me. If I hadn't been fool enough to listen to you all this time, I would have been in Berlin by now, completely healthy."

"But angel, what could we do? It was impossible—you know it was. And if you were to wait just one more month you'd be back on your feet, I'd settle my affairs and we'd take the children along…"

"The children are healthy. It is I who am ill."

"My friend, please understand—in this weather, if you should grow worse on the way… at least at home—"

"What? At least what? I'd die at home?" the sick woman cut in testily. But the word *die* had evidently frightened her and she gazed at her husband with a pleading, enquiring look. He lowered his eyes and kept silent. The sick woman's mouth suddenly twisted in a childish manner and tears began to flow down her cheeks. Her husband covered his face with a handkerchief and walked away from the carriage without saying a word.

"No, I am going," the sick woman declared, raised her eyes to the sky, folded her hands and began to whisper incoherent words. "My God, why? Why me?" she kept saying, and her tears flowed more freely. She prayed long and fervently but there was still the same pain, the same tightness in her chest; the sky, the fields and the road were just as grey and overcast; and the same autumn mist —no thicker, no thinner, but exactly the same—fell on the mud, on the roofs, on the carriage and on the sheepskin coats of the drivers, who chatted in strong, cheerful voices as they greased the wheels and harnessed a fresh team…

## II

The carriage was harnessed but the driver tarried. He went into the drivers' hut—a hot, stuffy, dark and oppressive place which smelt of humans, bread, cabbage and sheepskin. There were several drivers in the main room and a cook was busy at the stove, atop of which, covered in sheepskins, lay a sick man.

"Uncle Fyodor! Hey, Uncle Fyodor," said the driver—a young fellow in a sheepskin coat with a whip in his belt—as he entered the room and turned to the sick man.

"Whatcha need Fedya fer, numbskull?" one of the drivers replied. "Cantcha see yer carriage is waitin'?"

"Wanna ask him for his boots. Worn mine out," the young fellow answered, tossing back his hair and straightening the heavy gloves in his belt. "He sleepin'? Hey, Uncle Fyodor," he repeated, walking up to the stove.

"Whatcha want?" a weak voice said, and a gaunt, red-whiskered face looked down from the stove. A broad, emaciated hand, pale and hairy, pulled a drab coat over a bony shoulder clothed in a dirty shirt. "Gimme me a drink, brother… Whatcha want?"

The young fellow handed him a dipper filled with water.

"Fedya, listen," he said, shifting from foot to foot. "I reckon you won't be needin' them new boots… Maybe I could have 'em? Reckon you won't be walkin' no more."

Bending his weary head over the polished dipper, plunging his sparse, sagging moustaches in the water, the sick man drank weakly and greedily. His tangled beard was unclean and his dull, sunken eyes rose with difficulty to the young fellow's face. When he was done drinking he tried to lift a hand to his wet lips but he couldn't, so he wiped them off with the sleeve of his coat. Saying nothing and breathing heavily through his nose, he stared straight into the young fellow's eyes, gathering his strength.

"Maybe you promised 'em to someone else," said the fellow. "Then forget it. Only it's wet outside, and I've got a long ways to go, so I think to myself, I'll go and ask Fedya for his boots. I reckon he don't need 'em no more. But maybe you do—just say…"

Something overflowed and bubbled in the sick man's chest; he bent double, overtaken with a fit of choking, unrelenting, throaty coughing.

"Sure, he needs boots!" the cook suddenly bellowed for the whole hut to hear. "Hasn't left the stove for more 'n a month. Look at 'im, bustin' his guts—you know he's sick deep down inside when you hear him. Tell me, what's he need boots fer? They won't bury 'im in new ones. And it's high time for that, God forgive me… Look at 'im, bustin' his guts… Oughta put 'im in another hut, maybe… They got hospitals in town… But here he takes up the whole corner. Can't do a thing about it. Ain't got room to turn around—and they tell me to keep things neat…"

"Hey, Seryoga, get movin', will ya? People are waitin'," the drivers' headman shouted from the doorway.

Seryoga was ready to leave, but the sick man, still coughing, indicated with his eyes that he had an answer for him.

"You take the boots, Seryoga," he said, after suppressing the cough and catching his breath. "But when I die, buy me a stone, you hear?" he added hoarsely.

"Thank you, Uncle—I'll take the boots, then, and you'll get that stone."

"You heard him, fellas," the sick man managed to say, then again bent double and began to choke.

"Sure, we heard him," said one of the drivers. "You'd better go, Seryoga—the headman's comin' again. That Shirkinsky lady is in a bad way, you know."

Seryoga pulled off his torn, oversized boots in a hurry and tossed them under a bench. Uncle Fyodor's new boots fitted him perfectly, and he kept glancing down at them as he walked to the carriage.

"Fine-lookin' boots! Let me polish 'em," said the other driver, with brush in hand, as Seryoga climbed onto the box and picked up the reins. "Gave 'em up free, just like that?"

"Jealous, eh?" replied Seryoga, rising up and parting the bottom of his coat to show his feet. "Off you go, my dears!" he shouted at the horses, swinging his whip; and the carriage and barouche, with their passengers, bags and trunks, rolled off down the wet road and disappeared into the grey autumn mist.

The sick driver remained on the stove in the stuffy hut; unable to cough his lungs clear, he made a great effort to turn over on his other side and fell silent.

People came, went and ate in the hut all day long, while the sick man lay quiet. Before nightfall the cook climbed onto the stove and reached over his legs to get a sheepskin.

"Don't be cross with me, Nastasya," he said to her. "I'll quit your corner soon enough."

"Don't fret, nothin' we can do about it," muttered Nastasya. "But tell me, Uncle, what's the matter? Where does it hurt?"

"My insides is all rotten. God knows what it is."

"Your throat must be plenty sore, with all that coughin'…"

"Everything's sore. Death is coming—that's what it is. Oh…" the sick man groaned.

"Listen, you just cover up your legs like this," Nastasya said, pulling his coat over him as she climbed down from the stove.

Throughout the night a single light burned feebly in the hut. Nastasya and some ten drivers slept on the floor and benches, snoring loudly. The sick man alone kept groaning weakly, coughing and turning from side to side on the stove. Towards morning he fell completely silent.

"Had a strange dream last night," said the cook the next morning, stretching herself in the half-light. "I see Uncle Fyodor come down from the stove. He's goin' out to chop wood. 'Nastya,' he tells me, 'let me give you a hand.' And I say to him, 'You ain't fit to chop wood.' But he grabs hold of the axe and starts choppin'—swingin' and swingin'—all you see is chips flyin'. 'But you were sick,' I say. 'No,' he tells me, 'I'm all right.' Then he swings the axe so hard that it scares me… And I scream and wake up. You don't think he's dead, do ya? Uncle Fyodor! Hey, Uncle Fyodor!"

Fyodor did not respond.

"Might be… Let's have a look," said one of the drivers.

A thin arm covered with reddish hairs hung down from the stove; it was cold and pale.

"Go tell the stationmaster. Looks dead to me," said the driver.

Fyodor had no family—he had come from someplace else. On the following day they buried him in the new churchyard, beyond the woods, and for several days Nastasya kept telling everyone about her dream—how she had been the first to know that Uncle Fyodor was gone.

III

Spring had come. Murmuring streamlets flowed quickly down wet streets, wending their way among frozen clumps of dung; crowds bustled about in bright-coloured clothing, conversing in bright tones. The trees in little fenced-off gardens smelt of flower buds, and their boughs swayed lightly, barely audibly, in the fresh wind. Translucent droplets dripped and poured down every surface... Sparrows chirped tunelessly and flitted about on their tiny wings. On the sunny side of every street, on the fences, houses and trees, all was in motion, all sparkled. Joy and youth pervaded the sky, the earth and the heart.

On one of the main streets, in front of a large manor house, fresh straw had been scattered; inside the house lay the dying woman who had been so eager to go abroad.

By the closed door of her room stood her husband and a woman of mature years. A priest sat on a couch, keeping his eyes lowered and holding something wrapped in an *epitrachelion*.[1] In the corner, an old lady—the sick woman's mother—reclined in a Voltaire chair, weeping bitterly. One maid stood beside her with a clean handkerchief, waiting for the old lady to ask for it; another was rubbing something into her temples and blowing on the grey hair beneath her cap.

"Christ is with you, my friend," the husband said to the woman who stood by the door with him. "She has such trust in you… She listens to you… Please, persuade her, my dear—go on." He was about to open the door for the cousin, but she stopped him, dabbed at her eyes with a handkerchief and shook her head.

"I don't want her to see that I've been crying," she said and, opening the door herself, went into the room.

The husband was greatly agitated and seemed to be at his wits' end. He was about to approach the old lady, but stopped short, turned away and walked over to the priest on the other side of the room. The priest looked at him, raised his eyebrows heavenwards and sighed. His bushy, grey-flecked beard also rose and sank.

"My God, my God!" said the husband.

"What can we do?" the priest responded with a sigh, and again his eyebrows and beard rose and sank.

"And Mother," said the husband, almost in utter despair. "She cannot bear much more. To love someone—to love someone as she loves her… I just don't know. Father, if you could calm her down and persuade her to leave…"

The priest rose and went over to the old lady.

"Yes, a mother's heart is beyond price," he said, "but God is merciful."

The old lady's face suddenly began to twitch and she was seized with a hysterical hiccough.

"God is merciful," the priest continued when she had calmed down a little. "Let me say this, I had a sick man in my parish, much worse off than Marya Dmitrievna, and what do you know? A simple townsman cured him in no time, using nothing but herbs. And this very townsman is now in Moscow. I told Vasily Dmitrievich—worth trying, perhaps. If nothing else, it might console her. And with God, all things are possible."

"No, she won't live," said the old woman. "God will take her, when He should take me instead." And the hysterical hiccough grew so violent that she fainted away.

The sick woman's husband covered his face with his hands and ran out of the room.

The first person he saw in the corridor was his six-year-old boy, who was chasing his little sister with all his might.

"Shall I take the children to see their mother?" asked the nanny.

"No, she does not wish to see them. It would only upset her."

The boy halted for a minute, stared intently into his father's face, then suddenly stamped his foot and took off again with a cheerful cry.

"Daddy, she's a black horsey!" the boy shouted, pointing to his sister.

Meanwhile, in the bedroom, the cousin sat beside the sick woman and attempted, by skilfully directing the conversation, to prepare her for the thought of death. A doctor stood at one of the windows, mixing a draught.

The sick woman, in a white housecoat, was sitting up in bed, surrounded by pillows and gazing silently at her cousin.

"My friend," she cut in unexpectedly. "Don't try to prepare me. I am not a child. I am a Christian woman. I know all I need to know. I know I'm not long for this world. I know that if my husband had listened to me earlier I would have been in Italy and, possibly—no, certainly—would have been well by now. Everyone told him so. But what can one do? It must have been God's will. We are all guilty of many sins, I know—but I hope for God's mercy. We will all be forgiven—surely we will all be forgiven. I try to understand myself. I too am guilty of many sins, my friend—but I have suffered... How I have suffered... And I've tried to endure it patiently."

"Shall I summon the father, my friend? Receive the sacraments—your heart will feel all the lighter for it," said the cousin.

The sick woman bowed her head in token of consent.

"God, forgive me, a sinner," she whispered.

The cousin stepped out and winked a signal to the father.

"An angel," she said to the husband, with tears in her eyes.

The husband began to cry; the priest went through the door; the old lady remained unconscious; and silence descended on the antechamber. When five minutes had passed the priest emerged from the bedroom, removed his *epitrachelion* and arranged his hair.

"Thank the Lord, she is calmer now," he said. "She wishes to see you."

The cousin and husband entered the bedroom. The sick woman was crying softly as she gazed at the icon.

"Congratulations, my friend," said the husband.

"Thank you! I feel so good now—such a sweet, inexplicable feeling," the sick woman said as a faint smile played over her thin lips. "Oh, God is merciful! Isn't that true? He is merciful and all-powerful." And with an eager prayer she again fixed her tearful eyes on the icon.

Then, as if suddenly remembering something, she beckoned to her husband.

"You never want to do what I ask," she said in a weak, dissatisfied voice.

The husband, craning his neck, listened meekly.

"What is it, my friend?"

"How many times have I told you that these doctors don't know a thing? There are simple healers… They work wonders… The father was saying… A townsman… Send for him."

"For whom, my friend?"

"My God, he doesn't want to understand…" And the sick woman knit her brows and closed her eyes.

The doctor approached the bed and took her wrist. Her pulse was growing weaker and weaker. He winked a signal to the husband. The sick woman noticed this gesture and glanced about fearfully. Her cousin turned away and burst into tears.

"Don't cry. Don't torture us both," the sick woman told her. "You'll only rob me of my final comfort."

"You are an angel," said the cousin, kissing her hand.

"No, kiss me here—one only kisses the dead on the hand. My God, my God!"

That evening the sick woman was already a corpse, and the corpse lay in a coffin in the large home's parlour. Inside that large room, behind closed doors, a lector sat and intoned the psalms of David in a steady, nasal voice. Bright waxen light fell from tall silver candlesticks onto the pale brow of the deceased, onto the heavy waxen hands and the stony folds of the shroud that rose frightfully above the knees and toes. The lector read steadily, without understanding what he read, and in the quiet room his words sounded strange and died away slowly. Now and then the noise of children's voices and the patter of their feet wafted in from a distant room.

*Thou hidest Thy face, they are troubled: Thou takest away their breath, they die and return to their dust. Thou sendest forth Thy spirit, they are created: and Thou renewest the face of the earth. The glory of the Lord shall endure forever.*

The face of the deceased was stern, calm and dignified. There was no movement in the clean, cold brow or the firmly pressed lips. She was all attention. But did she at last grasp the meaning of these exalted words?

IV

The next month a stone chapel was erected over the grave of the deceased. There was still no stone above the grave of the driver, and only light-green grass sprouted through the mound that served as the only marker of the vanished existence of a human being.

"It'll be a sin, Seryoga," the cook at the post station said one day, "if you don't buy Fyodor a stone. You kept on sayin', 'It's winter, it's winter'—well, why can't you stick to your word now? I was there, I heard ya promise. He's already come back to ask for it once—you make him come back again, and he'll choke ya."

"I won't go back on my word," answered Seryoga. "I'll buy that stone. I said I will and I will—I'll buy it for a rouble and a half. I haven't forgotten. It's just that I've got to go and get it. Next time I'm in town, I'll buy it for sure."

"Could at least put a cross up," an old driver chimed in. "It's not right, I tell ya—wearin' them boots."

"Where am I supposed to get a cross? Can't hew it out of a log…"

"What're you talkin' about? Can't hew it out of a log, so take an axe and head out to the woods, bright and early, and hew it out there. Chop yourself down an ash tree. That'll make for a nice cross. Go early, or else you gotta get the watchman drunk. Can't be payin' in vodka for every damn thing. The other day I busted my whippletree, so I just went and chopped down a new one—nobody said a word."

Early the next morning, at first light, Seryoga took an axe and set out for the woods.

All was draped in a cool, dull shroud of still-falling dew, as yet untouched by the sun. The east was slowly growing brighter and its feeble light shone back from the wispy clouds covering the sky. Nothing stirred—not a single blade of grass below, not a single leaf on the uppermost branch of a tree. Only rarely did a beating of wings in a thicket or a rustling on the ground violate the wooded silence. Suddenly a strange sound, alien to nature, echoed and died away at the edge of the forest. But then it sounded again and was repeated steadily, over and over, down at the trunk of one of the motionless trees. One of the crowns began to tremble unusually, its juicy leaves began to whisper something and a redbreast that had been sitting on one of its branches fluttered up twice with a whistle and, twitching its tail, perched on another tree.

The noise of the axe below grew duller and duller, white chips, dripping with sap, flew onto the dewy grass and a faint crack was heard beneath the blows. The tree shuddered all over and leant to the side, then quickly straightened itself, shivering fearfully on its roots. For a moment all was still—but then the tree leant again, the crack sounded once more, and, snapping its boughs and lowering its branches, it fell, laying its crown on the damp earth. The noise of the axe and the footsteps subsided. The redbreast whistled and fluttered higher. The branch it had brushed with its wings swayed for a while and then stilled, as did the others. The trees displayed their splendour even more joyously, extending their motionless branches over the newly cleared space.

The first rays of the sun flashed through a passing cloud, then spread across the earth and the sky. Waves of mist rolled along the hollows, drops of dew sparkled on the foliage and translucent white clouds hurried over the blue expanse. Birds flitted about in the thicket, chirping happily, as if beside themselves; leaves full of sap whispered calmly and joyfully high above, and the branches of the living began to sway slowly, with dignity, over the dead, fallen tree.

# ALYOSHA THE POT

ALYOSHA WAS the younger brother. They nick-named him Pot because one day his mother sent him to the deacon's wife with a pot of milk, but he stumbled and fell, and the pot broke. His mother gave him a whipping and the boys teased him, called him "Pot". The nickname stuck—Alyosha the Pot.

Alyosha was a thin little fellow, lop-eared (his ears were like wings), with a big nose. The boys used to tease him, shouting, "Alyosha's nose is like a dog on a hill." There was a school in the village, but Alyosha didn't take to learning, and besides, he didn't have much time for it. His older brother had gone off to the big city to work for a merchant, so Alyosha had to help out his father from the time he was knee-high to a grasshopper. By the age of six he was out with his older sister in the pasture, looking after the sheep and the cow. Just a few years later he was watching the horses by day and by night. At twelve he was already ploughing and driving the cart. Didn't have much strength but he had plenty of skill. And he was always cheerful. When the boys made fun of him he either laughed or kept quiet. When his father bawled him out he kept quiet and listened; and as soon as his father was done he'd just smile and take up the chore that needed doing.

Alyosha was nineteen when his brother was taken for a soldier, and so his father placed him with the merchant instead. They gave Alyosha his brother's old boots, his father's hat and coat, and then drove him off to town. Alyosha was as pleased as could be with his new clothes, but the merchant didn't like what he saw.

"I thought you'd give me a man to take Simeon's place," he said, looking Alyosha up and down. "But you bring me this snot-nosed kid. What's he good for?"

"He can do anything, you'll see—harness the horses, drive 'em. Yes, he's a great one for work. He only looks weak as wicker, but he's all sinew inside."

"All right, we'll see."

"Best of all, he's meek as a lamb. Lives for work."

"Eh, what am I gonna do with ya? Leave 'im."

And so Alyosha came to live with the merchant.

The family was a small one: the merchant's wife, his old mother, his eldest son—married, brought up simply, now working with his father—and the other son, an educated fellow, who'd finished school and spent some time at the university, but was kicked out and now lived at home. And there was also the merchant's daughter, still a schoolgirl.

They didn't take to Alyosha at first. He was too much of a peasant—badly dressed, no manners, acting too familiar. But soon they got used to him. He was even better than his brother. He really was meek—did everything he was told, always willing, always quick, going from one task to another without stopping. Here at the merchant's, just as at home, all the work fell to Alyosha. The more he did, the more they piled onto his shoulders. The merchant's wife, the mother, the daughter, the son, the clerk and the cook, they all sent Alyosha running in every direction, forced him to do this, do that. All you ever heard in the house was, "Alyosha, run and fetch it! Get to it, Alyosha! Alyosha, did you forget? Mind you don't forget!" And Alyosha ran this way and that, forgot nothing, minded everything, got to it all and smiled the whole time.

He soon wore out his brother's boots; the merchant scolded him for walking about with his toes sticking out and ordered him to buy another pair at the market. Alyosha was happy with the new boots but he still had the same old feet, and he'd grow angry with them when they ached after a long day of running errands. And he was afraid his father would be vexed to learn, when he came to collect his wages, that the merchant had taken out the cost of the boots.

In the winter Alyosha would get up before dawn to chop the firewood, sweep out the yard, feed the cow and the horse, give them water. Then he would heat the stoves, polish the family's boots, clean their clothes and put out the samovars, making sure they were spick and span. Then the clerk might have him pull out the wares or the cook might have him knead the dough, clean the pots. Then he'd be sent out to deliver a message, or to bring the merchant's daughter home from school, or to get some oil for the old woman's lamp. "Where've you been, you damned fool?" one or another of them would ask him. "Why trouble yourself? Alyosha will get it. Alyosha! Hey, Alyosha!" And off he'd go.

He ate breakfast as he worked and rarely made it home in time for dinner. The cook scolded him for being missing at mealtimes, yet she felt sorry for him and would keep something hot for his dinner and supper. There was always more work at holiday time. The holidays made Alyosha especially happy because everyone would give him little tips. He'd never get more than sixty kopecks in all, but this was his money—he could spend it any way he liked. He never laid eyes on his wages. His father would come and take them from the merchant, and only chide Alyosha for wearing out his boots.

When he had saved up two roubles of this tip money, he took the cook's advice and bought himself a red knitted jacket. Putting it on brought him such joy that he couldn't close his mouth.

Alyosha was never much of a talker, and when he did speak he was always abrupt and brief. Whenever he was told to do something, or asked whether he could do this or that, he would always say, without the slightest hesitation, "Sure can"—and then he'd set about doing it until it was done.

He knew no prayers. He'd forgotten the ones his mother had taught him. And yet he prayed every morning and every evening—prayed with his hands, crossing himself.

Alyosha lived like this for a year and a half, and then, in the second part of the second year, came the most extraordinary event of his life. This was when he learnt, to his great surprise, of the possibility of a special sort of relationship between people, a relationship not based on material need. This happens when a person isn't needed just to polish another's boots, deliver a package or harness a horse. It happens when a person is needed for no reason at all—when another human being simply feels the need to serve and to caress the person. And now he, Alyosha, was that person. He made this discovery thanks to the cook, Ustinia. She was an orphan, still a young girl, and just as hardworking as Alyosha. She began to feel sorry for Alyosha, and for the first time in his life he sensed that he—not his services, but he himself—was needed by another human being. He never paid any mind to his mother feeling sorry for him; that was just natural, like him feeling sorry for himself. But here was Ustinia, a perfect stranger, who felt sorry for him. Here she was, saving him porridge with butter in a pot and watching him eat, her chin propped on her bare arm. And if he looked up at her she'd laugh, and he'd laugh too.

This was all so strange and so new that at first it frightened Alyosha. He felt it might get in the way of his work. Still, he was happy—and whenever he looked down at the trousers Ustinia had darned for him he'd shake his head and smile. He'd often think of her while working or running errands and would say to himself, "Ustyusha…" She used to help him whenever she could, and he would help her. She told him all about her life—how she lost her parents, how her aunt took her in and then sent her to work in town, how the merchant's son had tried to tempt her and how she had warded him off. Ustinia liked to talk and Alyosha liked to listen. He knew these things happened often enough: peasants coming to town for work and getting married to cooks. Then one time Ustinia asked if his parents meant to marry him off soon. He told her he didn't know, and that he didn't want to marry any of the village girls anyway.

"So who've you got your eye on?" she asked.

"I'd take you. Would you like that?"

"Look at you, Pot—you sure came right out with it!" she said, slapping him on the back with a *rushnik*.[1] "Well, why not?"

At Shrovetide, Alyosha's old man came to town to collect his son's wages. The merchant's wife had got wind of Alyosha's plan to marry Ustinia and didn't like it one bit. *Girl will get pregnant before you know it*, she thought. *Of what use will she be with a child?* So she told her husband.

The merchant gave Alyosha's father the money.

"Well, how's my boy getting along?" asked the peasant. "Told you, didn't I? He's a meek one."

"Meek he may be, but he's got a fool notion in his head. Wants to take our cook for a wife. And I'm not about to keep married servants. Won't have it."

"That fool! What's he thinking?" said the father. "Don't you worry, I'll straighten him out."

The peasant came into the kitchen and sat down at the table to wait for his son. Alyosha was out running errands and came back out of breath.

"I thought you had some sense in you! What's this you're planning?" the father asked.

"Nothin'…"

"What nothin'? You think you're gettin' married! I'll marry you off when the time's right, and to a proper girl of my choosing, not some town harlot."

The father talked and talked. Alyosha stood there and sighed. When the father was done, Alyosha smiled.

"Suppose we'll just drop it."

"You'd better."

After his father left and Alyosha was alone with Ustinia (she'd been listening outside the door), he said to her, "It's no go. You hear 'im? He's as cross as two sticks. Won't let us."

Ustinia wept silently into her apron. Alyosha clicked his tongue.

"Got to do as we're told. No choice."

In the evening, when the merchant's wife summoned him to close the shutters, she asked, "Have you done as your father told you and dropped all this nonsense?"

"Sure have," said Alyosha and gave a laugh, then broke into tears.

Alyosha never spoke to Ustinia about marriage again, and went on living as before.

One day the clerk sent him up to clear the snow off the roof. He climbed up, scraped it clean, and was prying frozen clumps from the gutters when he lost his footing and fell, still holding the shovel. He had the bad luck to land not in the snow, but on the iron threshold. Ustinia ran up to him, along with the merchant's daughter.

"Alyosha, you hurt?"

"Hurt nothin'…"

He wanted to get up, but he couldn't, so he smiled instead. They carried him off to his little shed. A doctor's assistant came to look him over and asked where the pain was.

"Everywhere, but it's nothin'. Only thing is, master won't be happy. And better send word to Pa."

Alyosha lay there for two days. On the third day they called in the priest.

"You really dying?" asked Ustinia.

"Sure I am. Can't live forever. We've all got to go sometime," Alyosha said, speaking quickly, as usual. "Thank you, Ustyusha. Thank you for feeling sorry for me. Good thing they didn't let us marry. Nothin' would've come of it. Worked out for the best."

He prayed with the priest, using only his hands and his heart. And what he felt in his heart was this: just as it's good down here when you obey and do no harm, so will it be up there.

He didn't speak much after that. He'd only ask for water now and then, and he kept looking surprised.

Something surprised him, and he stretched out and died.

# NOTES

TRANSLATOR'S PREFACE

1    Luckily, an especially engaging brief introduction, Donna Orwin's *Simply Tolstoy*, has recently been published (New York: Simply Charly, 2017).

2    Mark Aldanov's *The Riddle of Tolstoy* (*Zagadka Tolstogo*) (Berlin: Izdatel'stvo I.P. Ladyznikova, 1923; reprinted, Providence, RI: Brown University Press, 1969), which has never been translated into English, remains an indispensable critical—in every sense of the word—guide to Tolstoy's thought. Aldanov's fellow émigré, Ivan Bunin, engages with his analysis of the question of death in Tolstoy's work in *The Liberation of Tolstoy: A Tale of Two Writers*, which has been translated and edited by Thomas Gaiton Marullo and Vladimir T. Khmelkov (Evanston, IL: Northwestern University Press, 2001), p. 129 and *passim*.

3    Much has been written about this novella. An excellent place to start is *Tolstoy's* The Death of Ivan Il'ich:

*A Critical Companion*, ed. Gary R. Jahn (Evanston, IL: Northwestern University Press, 1999).

4    The Russian name of Tolstoy's titular horse is "Kholstomer"—literally, "one who measures linen", a phrase that doesn't sound much like the name of a horse in English. He is called Kholstomer on account of his long, regular stride; his gait, in other words, could be used to measure lengths of linen. In their excellent early translation, Louise and Aylmer Maude call the horse "Strider". Their solution is very effective indeed, even though it now brings to mind the work of another big T: Tolkien. I have opted for "Pace-setter", which suggests impressive speed and regularity, while at the same time foreshadowing the horse's fate: he isn't meant to win. Like the measurer of linen, a pace-setter is a common worker, not a member of the elite. And by telling his life story in slow, measured tones, Pace-setter also adjusts the pace of the younger, friskier horses around him, who stand still and listen in awe.

5    It's not by chance that Viktor Shklovsky cites the story as one of the key examples of Tolstoy's use of "defamiliarization", the device of making the familiar strange, which the critic and his formalist colleagues regarded as central to literary art. See *Theory of the Prose*, translated by Benjamin Sher, introduction by Gerald L. Buns (Normal, IL: Dalkey Archive Press, 1991).

6    D.S. Mirsky, *A History of Russian Literature from Its Beginnings to 1900*, ed. Francis J. Whitfield (Evanston, IL: Northwestern University Press, 1999), p. 321.

## THE DEATH OF IVAN ILYICH

1    Introduced by Peter the Great in 1722—and abolished by the Bolsheviks in 1917—the Table of Ranks was an official list of fourteen ranks and positions of the civil, military, and court systems of imperial Russia. The tenth rank of the civil service was that of collegiate secretary.

2    E.F. Charmeur was one of the finest tailors in St Petersburg in the late imperial period.

3    Donon's was an exclusive restaurant in St Petersburg at the time.

4    An official for special assignments was a position for imperial civil servants of the sixth to the ninth ranks. (See note 1.)

5    Old Believers are Eastern Orthodox Christians who refuse to accept the reforms to the rituals and practices of the Church implemented by Patriarch Nikon between 1652 and 1666. Although they were heavily persecuted in both the imperial and Soviet periods, communities of Old Believers survive to this day.

6 Named after Maria Feodorovna, the second wife of Emperor Paul I, the Institutions of Empress Maria was a government office in imperial Russia that managed hospitals, orphanages, poorhouses, homes for the disabled and educational facilities for women and children. It was abolished in 1917.

7 A line from the poem "Song" (1796) by Yury Neledinsky-Meletsky (1751–1828).

8 Johann Gottfried Karl Christian Kiesewetter (1766–1819) played an important role in popularizing the philosophy of Immanuel Kant and was the author of an influential textbook of logic, *Grundriß einer reinen allgemeinen Logik, nach Kantischen Grundsätzen*, which first appeared in 1791 and went through several editions.

9 A men's hairstyle named after the French operatic tenor Victor Capoul (1839–1924), in which the hair is parted down the middle with two curls on either side of the forehead.

PACE-SETTER: THE STORY OF A HORSE

1 The plot of this story was first conceived by Mikhail Aleksandrovich Stakhovich (1819–1858), a writer and musician who collected and published Russian folk tales and folk songs.

2     Founded by Count Alexei Grigoryevich Orlov-Chesmensky (1737–1808) in 1776, the Khrenovoye stud farm in Voronezh Province is still in operation today.

3     German: "Bring another box. There are two there."

## THREE DEATHS

1     The *epitrachelion* is the narrow, richly embroidered stole worn by Orthodox and Eastern Catholic priests and bishops as a symbol of their priesthood. The object wrapped in the epitrachelion is an icon.

## ALYOSHA THE POT

1     *Rushnik*: a type of embroidered towel traditionally used in East Slavic religious rituals and ceremonies such as weddings and funerals.

# TRANSLATOR'S
# ACKNOWLEDGEMENTS

I thank Adam Freudenheim, Rory Williamson, India Darsley and the Pushkin Press team for commissioning and editing this translation, and for placing it between such attractive covers. Seán Costello's careful, sensitive copyediting improved the text immeasurably. Insightful, generous comments from Maria Bloshteyn, Robert Chandler, Anne Marie Croft, Caryl Emerson, Roman Koropeckyj, Stephanie Malak, Irina Mashinski, Donna Orwin, Vadim Shneyder, Irene Yoon and, especially, Oliver Ready clarified my vision at crucial moments. My mother, Anna Glazer, gave me help, advice, and encouragement throughout my journey with Tolstoy. And my deepest thanks are owed to my wife, Jennifer Croft, for her brilliance and infinite patience.

# PUSHKIN PRESS

Pushkin Press was founded in 1997, and publishes novels, essays, memoirs, children's books—everything from timeless classics to the urgent and contemporary.

This book is part of the Pushkin Collection of paperbacks, designed to be as satisfying as possible to hold and to enjoy. It is typeset in Monotype Baskerville, based on the transitional English serif typeface designed in the mid-eighteenth century by John Baskerville. It was litho-printed on Munken Premium White Paper and notch-bound by the independently owned printer TJ International in Padstow, Cornwall. The cover, with French flaps, was printed on Rives Linear Bright White paper. The paper and cover board are both acid-free and Forest Stewardship Council (FSC) certified.

Pushkin Press publishes the best writing from around the world—great stories, beautifully produced, to be read and read again.

STEFAN ZWEIG · EDGAR ALLAN POE · ISAAC BABEL
TOMÁS GONZÁLEZ · ULRICH PLENZDORF · JOSEPH KESSEL
VELIBOR ČOLIĆ · LOUISE DE VILMORIN · MARCEL AYMÉ
ALEXANDER PUSHKIN · MAXIM BILLER · JULIEN GRACQ
BROTHERS GRIMM · HUGO VON HOFMANNSTHAL
GEORGE SAND · PHILIPPE BEAUSSANT · IVÁN REPILA
E.T.A. HOFFMANN · ALEXANDER LERNET-HOLENIA
YASUSHI INOUE · HENRY JAMES · FRIEDRICH TORBERG
ARTHUR SCHNITZLER · ANTOINE DE SAINT-EXUPÉRY
MACHI TAWARA · GAITO GAZDANOV · HERMANN HESSE
LOUIS COUPERUS · JAN JACOB SLAUERHOFF
PAUL MORAND · MARK TWAIN · PAUL FOURNEL
ANTAL SZERB · JONA OBERSKI · MEDARDO FRAILE
HÉCTOR ABAD · PETER HANDKE · ERNST WEISS
PENELOPE DELTA · RAYMOND RADIGUET · PETR KRÁL
ITALO SVEVO · RÉGIS DEBRAY · BRUNO SCHULZ · TEFFI
EGON HOSTOVSKÝ · JOHANNES URZIDIL · JÓZEF WITTLIN